Tales from the Greenwood District

A PEEK INTO BLACK WALL STREET ... BEFORE THE MASSACRE

Tales from the Greenwood District

A PEEK INTO BLACK WALL STREET ... BEFORE THE MASSACRE

JULIAN B. WADDELL

"I came not to Tulsa as many came, lured by the dream of making money and bettering myself in the financial world, but because of the wonderful cooperation I observed among our people, and especially the harmony of spirit and action that existed between the businessmen and women."

~ Mary E. Jones Parrish
1921

Doomsday Banana, LLC.
645 Wynn Dr. NW. #5331
Huntsville, AL 35814

Ordering Information:

Orders by U.S. trade bookstores and wholesalers. Quantity sales. Special discounts are available on quantity purchases by corporations, associations, and others. For details, contact the publisher at the following email address: create@doomsdaybanana.com

Connect with Julian B. Waddell:

Instagram:
Instagram.com/IdeaWingman

LinkedIn:
LinkedIn.com/in/ideawingman

ISBN: 978-1-7371319-0-8

Tale 404 is a series of stories that will continue to edutain* you even after you've finished with this book. Scan the QR code to access little-known historical stories and explore the rarely discussed intersection of seemingly unrelated occurrences.

Edutain is a word.

Dedication

*I dedicate this book to my aunt, **Dorothy Waddell Towns**. I had so many questions I wanted to ask you …*

*I've been working on iterations of this book since the launch of the Reading Rainbow Young Writers and Illustrators Contest in 1995 (special shoutout to Levar Burton and PBS), but I couldn't have finished this book without **Sharee Moore** keeping me on track.*

*A very special thanks to my **mom**, who encouraged me to become the best me that I could be. To my **dad,** who not only got me into history but got me into deep diving, connecting the historical dots, and storytelling. To my **grandparents** who never steered away from teaching our history without sugarcoating it. To my **siblings** (blood-related or not), who always go above and beyond to help me shine. To my **aunts** and **uncles**, who've always stood in as my second parents. And, most importantly, to **<u>Janna Peterson</u>**, the most spectacular person I know and the reason I am the unstoppable force I am today.*

Contents

Author's Note

This book is not about the Black Wall Street **Massacre.** I won't be the author of another story that adds to the weight you already feel about the racial trauma most of us navigate each day. We already know the depth of race-based stress, and we're worn out by the media's negative portrayal of minorities. Yes, we're tired of viewing the deaths of unarmed Black men, women, and children at the hands of those who've been sworn to protect and serve. We're tired of watching on our screens as Black lives are interrupted by shootings, chokings, and modern-day lynchings. We all read stories about our fallen ones and even witnessed how they died; we swore never to stop saying their names.

There are countless people like Philando, Trayvon, Tamir, John, Breonna, Atatiana, Ahmaud, Botham, and George. I want you to think about what their futures could have been had their lives not been interrupted. Those are the thoughts that inspired me to write this book. I imagined them in that bubble of time and how they each had a story full of joy, pain, adventures, sorrows, love, and loss ahead of them. They had dreams!

Just like them, there was a time **before** the massacre on Black Wall Street. I want to talk to you about those days when the Greenwood District was a haven for Black people. Through the character sketches in this book, I want you to view life through the eyes of Jean, Annalie, Shelton, Marie, Julius, Jeremiah, Eli, Jordan, and Eddie. I want you to laugh with them and cry. I want you to share in their mishaps and triumphs. I want you to imagine them in this snapshot of time before their lives were interrupted. Then I want you to decide to live your own life.

YOU'RE AN OVERCOMER/DESTINED FOR GREATNESS

As kids, many of us had a favorite superhero. We grew up imagining ourselves with the special powers of our favorite costumed crusader. We wanted to fly like they could. Or we wanted to be invincible with super strength. We wanted to have X-ray vision, invisibility, or superspeed. The reason why is because those superhuman abilities would help us defeat the bad guys, be the hero, and save the day. But I need you to be confident that you can do and be just that. You can be a hero by changing the world around you. When you see a problem that needs to be solved, you can be the solution. I want you to be confident that those heroic feats are not far-fetched at all. Maybe you can't see through walls, but you can see the solution to the problems in our world; you can BE the solution. You are the solution! You are destined for greatness, so let's go change the world.

As you read these *Tales from the Greenwood District*, remind yourself that each day is a gift. It's your opportunity to live out something bigger and brighter than what faces you today. When you arrive at your final destination, the real headline is how you lived. When and how you died is just the footnote.

We rise together,
Julian B. Waddell

Foreword

On April 20, 2021, former police officer, Derek Chauvin, was convicted for murdering George Floyd. Floyd, like me, was Black. Like many Black people before him, and many after, he had perished unnecessarily at the hands of the police. But this was different. Floyd's killer had been punished. However, in 33 years of life, I had only seen this happen once before. Dare I feel hope? Could this be the beginning of a new era of police accountability? I was allowed to ponder the possibilities of change for but a few hours before hope was stolen from me.

Democratic Majority Leader Nancy Pelosi gave a speech addressing the conviction. Two minutes and fifteen seconds in, she said, "Thank you, George Floyd, for sacrificing yourself for justice." My blood boiled. George Floyd did not sacrifice himself for anything. He was not a martyred civil rights leader. He didn't lay his life down on the frontlines of injustice. All he did was try to buy something at a store. The clerk thought the twenty-dollar bill he used was fake and called the police. The police came and murdered him. Tell me, where was the sacrifice?

Human beings love to frame history within narratives. By doing this, we can look back and see clear lines between right and wrong, heroes and villains. But so much is lost in this reductive reframing of the past. On April 20th, Derek Chauvin was recast as a villain and Floyd as a hero. The villain gets punished. The hero rises above it all to become a symbol of something or whatever. Everything else is lost.

There has never been a day in my life where I wanted to sacrifice myself for anything, let alone the ambiguous concept of justice. Today, I woke up and went to the store because I wanted raspberries for my yogurt. If someone had told me that this desire would lead to me dying in a viral video, I would have stayed home and ate plain yogurt. I think George Floyd would've made a similar choice. He and I are people, not symbols, heroes, or hashtags. We have our own hopes and dreams for ourselves, and we do not want to be reframed in history so that the tragedy of a life lived under oppression is easier to digest.

If we looked back 100 years, I imagine the Black residents of Tulsa, Oklahoma would share this sentiment. One hundred years from the moment that I am writing this, the citizens of Tulsa are just starting their day. For the next few weeks, they will go about their lives just like you and me. In less than a month, many of them will be dead. But if we focus only on that, we rob them of their humanity. We do to them what history is doing to George Floyd and define them by the worst thing that ever happened to them. So let's not do that.

Let us take a moment to remember the names of those who have passed. Let us take a moment to see them as more than victims, casualties, or statistics. Let us meditate on their thoughts, empathize with their dreams, and remember them as they were. Remember them as you and I are right now—alive.

Justin Collier Mickens
Executive Producer
Fancy Logo Films

Introduction

It's the summer of 1918, and a devastating second wave of the Spanish flu pandemic was hitting America. You see, the first World War was coming to an end, and people at home were tired of self-quarantining. Returning soldiers, who were infected with the disease, were also spreading it to the general population. There wasn't a vaccine or even an approved plan for how to reduce the flu's spread, especially for those in densely-populated cities. Hundreds of thousands of people were dying in cities across America. The final death toll reached fifty million worldwide and 675,000 in the U.S.

Responsibility to make the decisions and improvise plans needed to safeguard U.S. citizens fell to local mayors and health officials. Not to mention, there was a lot of pressure on people to appear patriotic. After all, it was wartime. So with the media downplaying the disease's spread, many bad decisions slipped through undetected. To make matters worse, the second wave of deadly influenza was worse than the first.

TULSA, OKLAHOMA

In Oklahoma, 7,350 people died of influenza and related infections in the six months between October 1, 1918, and April 1, 1919. In October alone, the *Tulsa Democrat* (predecessor of *The Tulsa Tribune*) recorded 200 flu deaths in a story printed November 3, 1918.

Tulsa Red Cross officials, doctors, and city officials gathered for an emergency meeting on October 7, 1918 in order to mobilize resources. While all this was happening, everyone expected the poorest part of the population to suffer the most. Historian and professor, Alfred Crosby, noted that the Black population, who were expected to have higher influenza infections and deaths, actually had *lower* rates than the white population during the same time. This was not the norm. Some believe that this shift had a lot to do with socioeconomic factors at the time. During this time, Black Tulsans existed in a thriving community dubbed the Greenwood District, also commonly known as "Black Wall Street."

Also notable during that time period was the thought process of African American soldiers returning from war. They had expected to come home heroes; however, Black soldiers received a rude awakening upon their return. As these veterans tried to re-enter the labor market following World War I, social tensions and anti-Black sentiment increased in cities with high job competition. At the same time, Black veterans also pushed to have their civil rights enforced because they believed they had earned full citizenship through their military service.

But let's take a step back.

A RACIST PRESIDENT

Woodrow Wilson was the first Southerner and, at the time, the only candidate from a former Confederate state to be elected president since before the Civil War. His ascension to the presidency was celebrated by Southerners who believed in segregation. Several historians have looked at public records to spotlight consistent examples of Wilson's overtly racist policies and political appointments. For example, he appointed staunch segregationists in his Cabinet, who then guided the policies of the president's executive departments.

D. W. Griffith's film *The Birth of a Nation* (1915) was a catalyst that helped set the tone for white supremacy in America. It didn't help matters that Wilson chose it as the first motion picture to be screened in the White House. The film presents a stereotype-laden portrayal of African Americans as sexually aggressive toward white women. It also depicts African Americans as unintelligent, even as actors in blackface often carried out these depictions. In contrast, the film presents the Ku Klux Klan

(KKK) as critical in the preservation of American values and a social order where white supremacy rules. Some historians have said that the movie was so popular that it increased enrollments in the KKK.

While all this was happening, there was the Great Migration of African Americans out of the South in 1917 and 1918. The surge was in response to the demand for industrial labor related to the war. However, this migration sparked race riots, including the East St. Louis riots of 1917. The public mounted a vigorous objection and Wilson responded by asking the attorney general if the federal government could intervene. He called the riots "disgraceful outrages." However, Attorney General Thomas Watt Gregory advised Wilson not to take direct action against the riots.

In 1920, it was the end of Woodrow Wilson's second term, and most Progressives rejoined the Republican Party. They expected their former leader, Theodore Roosevelt, to make a third run for the presidency. He was the overwhelming favorite for the Republican nomination; however, those plans ended when Roosevelt suddenly died on January 6, 1919.

As a result, Warren G. Harding ran on the platform of normalcy because of all the things happening during that time. He called for restoration and "normalcy" as a way to calm America's turbulent waters.

CONNECTING THE DOTS

- Northeastern Oklahoma was in an economic slump that increased unemployment.
- The Greenwood District flourished and drew large numbers of Black Americans.
- Racial tensions and fears existed amidst a deadly pandemic.

So, here comes Dick Rowland, the young Black man whose story sparked the downfall of the illustrious Greenwood District. Dick Rowland was a nineteen-year-old Black shoe shiner who startled Sarah Paige, a seventeen-year-old elevator operator. The reports about what actually happened vary. In general, Rowland tripped in an elevator on his way to a segregated bathroom. Another white store clerk reported the incident as an "assault" or a rape. It's important to note that Sarah herself said that she was not assaulted or raped. Despite this, Dick Rowland was promptly arrested for the crime.

As it was in those days, after the young man was arrested, a lynch mob gathered outside the courthouse where he was being held. News got back to the local Black population. When they heard that Dick Rowland was going to be lynched, they arrived at the courthouse, too. The night ended in a fight between the lynch mob and armed African Americans, some of whom were WWI veterans. Shots were fired and twelve people were killed: ten whites and two Blacks. The incident highlighted the height of racial fear of that time.

Dick Rowland wasn't killed. He left Tulsa soon after that night.

THE TULSA MASSACRE

Late at night on May 31, 1921, mobs of white men retaliated by sparking a riot that lasted sixteen hours, during which time they started fires and U.S. planes dropped firebombs. These were the first records of bombs hitting U.S. soil. Between that night and the next day, angry white mobs leveled thirty-five city blocks of the Greenwood District, displaced thousands of residents, and killed hundreds. Official reports from the Oklahoma Bureau of Labor and Statistics state that thirty-nine people died: twenty-six Blacks and thirteen whites. However, a state commission gives a death toll ranging from 75-300 dead. Many of the Greenwood District residents were never seen or heard from again.

Tales from the Greenwood District is a series of short fictional stories that add color and dimension to Black Wall Street *before* the Tulsa Massacre. Despite the death, danger, and devastation around every turn, this exclusive Black society still thrived. Each tale shows depth to who we are as a people, our culture, and our shared happiness and pain.

YOU'LL READ THE TALES OF:

- A nurse who avoids grieving a sudden loss in the midst of battling the deadly Spanish flu …

- A returning Army veteran who fights his inner demons while looking for purpose … yet his journey takes an unexpected turn …

- A grandson who goes on a walking tour of the Greenwood District with his grandmother, which not only reveals the founders' stories but also a secret about himself …

- A white Tulsa resident wrestling with the mounting tensions of the angry mobs just one day before they embark on their historic killing spree …

- Teenagers who re-discover important truths and better understand the meaning of life and enduring friendship …

- A WWI veteran who demonstrates his commitment to sacrifice even in the face of unexpected danger …

- Former slaves owned by Native Americans who learn more about the American dream than anyone ever believed possible …

- A single mother of two who defies the odds and learns new ways to turn the impossible into what's possible …

- A white American Red Cross official who must make a harrowing choice … If caught in the act, the consequences could cost her more than just her job …

Eli and Jordan

Two friends uncover important revelations about their futures and themselves …

The Lincoln Motion Picture Company in Omaha, Nebraska was founded by George and Nobel Johnson in 1916. Aimed at African American audiences, it was the first all-Black movie production unit in America. The company created five films, which were shown in Black churches and assembly halls.

MAY 30, 1921

Eli hid a smile before shooting a hot look of disgust at the young boy peeping through the cracked bedroom door.

"I oughta bop you on the head for spying!" Eli quipped.

"Daddy said you should help me with breakfast when mother isn't well," Stephon said as he eased the door open.

"Well, where's he at so we can ask him about that now?" Eli made a great show of searching the room. Stephon's lips puckered into a baby scowl.

"You know you're lucky you're my brother, right?" Eli reminded Stephon.

"You can have an apple and some buttered toast this morning before school," Eli said.

Stephon looked at Eli from head to toe. "First of all, we don't even have school today. But why are you wearing *that*?"

"You just worry about getting your knobby head to school on time this morning! I have a thing, so can't walk you today." Eli spoke quickly and dipped out the door before Stephon could protest.

∞

Eli set out in the direction of Booker T. Washington High School and thought, *I've been holding this news in my heart for so long. I gotta tell somebody TODAY.*

The sky was clear as Eli neared the three-story brick building of the school. Eli thought, *Jordan better not chicken out like last time. I'm ready to share my secret ... tomorrow I plan to ...*

"What are you wearing?" Jordan asked quizzically while staring at Eli.

"Applesauce! I look good," Eli retorted confidently.

"You look like a dewdropper," Jordan chortled.

"A spiffy dewdropper, though. But enough about me. I can't believe *mister* Jordan is skipping schooling. I guess your mom is right. I *am* a bad influence," Eli teased.

"Close your head, Eli. There's no school on Memorial Day! Today *is* the day that you will always look back fondly on when you think about why you *stayed here* and made it big on Negro Wall Street."

Stephon's big head was right about school! My little sis, Anna, wouldn't have mixed up the days like this. She was the caretaker. She was the one who held things together. She was also the one taken by the Spanish flu. Eli cut off the sad thoughts; instead, offering Jordan a testy reply.

"I doubt that! Maybe it's more like the day *you* decide to take the train to Hollywood with ME. With your business mind and my talent, we could be bigger than even the Lincoln Motion Picture Company!" Eli stood tall; feet widely planted and arms folded matter-of-factly.

There was a brief awkward silence before Jordan put his arm around Eli's shoulder and said, "Let's blouse."

The two meandered down E. Easton Street in search of one final adventure together before the summer really began. Underneath all the playful banter, Jordan knew that today he only had one shot to convince Eli to stay in Greenwood. And he couldn't mess it up.

☙

Usually if there was some mischief to get into, it was Eli pulling Jordan along for the ride. This time, Eli thought it would be fun to let Jordan take the lead. *But first ...*

"Jo, if we actually had schooling to skip, we mighta picked the worst day ever because literally most of downtown is closed! But let's go behind Jacy's Bakery to see if they put those boxes of cakes, rolls, and the fancy French things out this morning!" Eli started skipping off in the direction of the bakery.

"Uh, Eli, those French things are called *croissants*. And how did you know they put out bread all like that? They have gingersnap cookies, too?" Jordan ran, but just a little, in order to catch up. Some might say he is short for his age, but that didn't bother Jordan one bit. From an early age, he knew it wasn't his body that would push him to greatness; it was his mind. Actually, it was Jordan's studious nature that caused the wild and adventurous Eli to seek out his friendship almost seven years ago.

Jordan couldn't forget that day. It was after school on Tuesday, September 8, 1914. There was this big old tree he liked to sit and read under near where the other kids played hopscotch, leapfrog, skipping games, and, of course, marbles. He had just finished a chapter of *The Call of the Wild* and planned to squeeze in a chapter of *The Wonderful Wizard of Oz* before heading home to do chores.

That's when George Harper walked up and said, "Why do you sit over here with a bunch of dumb books?" Before Jordan could reply, George asked, "Why don't you play with the rest of us?" Tiny beads of sweat formed on George's nose. He didn't bother wiping them away. Before Jordan could figure out what was going on, George reached over and slapped the books out of his hands and into the dirt at the base of the tree. Jordan's mouth hung open as he looked at his precious books through a rising cloud of dust.

Just like that, Eli strode over and decked ole George Harper right in the face! Before that day, Eli hadn't even said much to Jordan, but he still remembers Eli's words to George.

"You better recognize who you're messing with, George! One day, Jordan is gonna be the best doctor that Greenwood has ever seen! If you mess with him, you mess with me!" Eli stared down at George, who, at that point, could only squint with his one good eye. That was in second grade. The two have been inseparable ever since.

Jordan smiled at the memory, but his teeth practically fell out of his head when he saw Eli sorting through the boxes of sweets piled behind Jacy's. They smelled so good, and it looked like they weren't the only ones grabbing breakfast pastries. There was Ms. Alice, who worked down at the market. Oh, and there was Johnny. Everybody knew him.

"Hey, J! What's good?" Eli greeted Johnny. Eli always came up with nicknames for people.

"Sup, Eli. Getting my morning grub before I get new threads down at the Drexel on Main. You know I always gotta look cold as ice on Saturday nights." Johnny already looked cool as he smoothed the front of his jacket. He did some fancy footwork, twirled once, and tipped his hat before he walked off. Jordan made a mental note to remember that dance move for later.

"I bet that brotha knows how to parlay with the ladies!" Eli said with a laugh.

"Well, I just think a *real* lady wouldn't want somebody just telling her what she wants to hear," Jordan said.

"What you know about what the ladies want, Jo?" Eli grinned and busted out laughing.

"I know everything *you've* taught me, but the way you're dressed today has me rethinking everything I ever learned from you, Eli!" The two elbowed each other and laughed together as they meandered down the narrow street behind Jacy's.

"You might can get away with insulting *me*, but don't try that with your girlfriend … if you can even find one around here!" Eli said with a laugh.

"Listen, I'm trying to tell you. This place ain't it whether you're looking for a wife or a career. Literally, the world is ours for the taking! Why limit all that brainpower to a small section of town in a little ole city like Tulsa?" Eli persisted.

"I just think that Greenwood is full of lawyers, doctors, and engineers. Then we have hoteliers and businessmen who are some of the brightest around. You won't find talent like this in Atlanta, Chicago, New York, or … Los Angeles," Jordan said.

"I've done my research, too, Jo. You're talking about MEN. What about opportunities for women? You want a wife who is allowed to do more than sew clothes and bake cakes, don't you? That's all I see around here. So, if I ever have children, I want daughters who grow up in a place where there really are no limits. What about being a movie star? Or a pilot? Or even the mayor?" Eli's passionate speech reminded Jordan of the surprise he had in store.

"Let's go," Jordan said.

"So where are we going, Jo? The train station?" Eli tried to goad Jordan into a response.

«Close, but nope! We›re going to watch *The Green-Eyed Monster* up at Dreamland Theater," Jordan replied.

"Wait, wait, wait! How'd you pull that off?" Eli asked with a playful jab in Jordan's direction.

The Green-Eyed Monster was Eli's favorite movie. And even though it's been two years since it came out, Ms. Williams promised Jordan that she would show it today just for him.

"Before we see the motion picture, let's go out to the old trainyard. I'm ready to show you that I have just as much guts as you!" Jo told Eli.

"Wait!" Eli ran to catch up to Jordan. On the way to the old trainyard, they passed by a familiar house.

"Jo, let's stop here at my Aunt Rhesa's. You already know my older cousin, Shelton, always got something *good* in the back of his closet. He works over at the Stradford during the day, so ... It's on for you and me!" Eli said in an excited whisper.

There it was. Right there on the top shelf of Shelton's closet. The brown paper bag crinkled in their eager hands as they took a few swigs from the bottle half-filled with forbidden amber liquid. Jordan let out something that was a cross between a squeak and a squeal. Eli began to fan both hands toward their open mouths, but the liquid fire was true to its name and burned all the way down.

Suddenly, the screen door wheezed open then slammed closed with a *Whap!*

They looked at each other with wide eyes as Eli mouthed the words, "Aunt Rhesa's back!" A silent fit of giggles seemed to overtake the two as they tried to shush each other without actually making a sound.

Jordan jerked his head toward the door even as Eli used both hands to wildly gesture "no"! But Jordan was taking the lead today. He tumbled out of the closet with little to no dignity and made a run for the screen door. Eli was right behind him still choking back giggles. As the duo ducked around the corner, they could hear Aunt Rhesa call out, "Shelton? Is that you? Who's there?"

Jordan took off at a sprint with Eli hot on his heels. When they slowed to a stroll, he tossed Eli a croissant from the shoulder bag he always carried.

"You almost got us caught!" Eli accused through a barrage of throaty laughter.

"Just eat your French thing and let's get over to the trainyard before it's too late to catch our movie," Jordan said. "Oh, and your cap's on backwards, *bro*." he said with barely contained laughter.

Eli's smart-mouthed retort was interrupted by an authoritative voice.

"Hey, you kids, what are you doing out this far from town?"

They turned and saw Officer Pack coming their way. He was one of the District's few Negro police officers. Eli groaned quietly, but Jordan resisted the urge.

The trainyard was at the edge of town. The tracks marked one of the boundaries that separated Negroes and whites in Tulsa.

"Oh. You boys are headed in the direction of trouble," Officer Pack said sternly. "Hey, what's that

I smell?" he asked with his nose pointed in their direction.

"Officer, that's just this rum bread we got from Jacy's," Eli said quickly.

Officer Pack looked skeptical.

"Hey. I know you!" He pointed at Jordan. "You're the one who's on the Booker T. Washington Student Auxiliary Board and also the winner of the Oklahoma Science Lab Competition. Alright, son! You're going places!" Officer Pack exclaimed as he clapped Jordan on the shoulder.

"Things might feel easy for you here. But I'm from Chicago, and the world is a very different place than in Greenwood," Officer Pack warned. "I don't want you to let your guard down around here and think that the world is going to treat you as kindly as it does in Greenwood."

"Yes, sir!" Eli and Jordan said in unison.

"I had to work hard for everything I've been able to have here. Nothing was given to me for free. That's why, although I'm one of two Negroes policing these here streets, I'll always be known as one of the first of our kind to do so. Boys, ain't nothing free in this world. You gotta work for it. Now keep that in mind as you finish up your schooling. *Ain't nothing free.* Now we gotta go, but stay outta trouble." Officer Pack said with raised brows. He waited for their responses before heading back to where his partner stood on the corner.

"Yes, sir!" the kids said again to his retreating back.

"Ain't nothing free, *boys*," Jordan twittered in Eli's ear.

"Okay, okay, okay! Enough with the *boy* and *bro*, will ya?" Eli snapped.

"This is exactly why I can't wait to get out of this town! I *will* go to Hollywood, where I can wear pants, be a big shot film director, live on this side of the tracks *or* the other … *and* be called by the name my momma gave me—Elizabeth Ann Ferguson! Do you know the last thing my daddy told me before he disappeared? He said, 'Elizabeth, you can do anything you make up your mind to do,'" Eli said before quietly adding, "even leave here."

Eli balanced carefully on the tracks and inched towards the bridge where they liked to sit and dangle their feet off the side. Jordan had a carefully prepared speech about why he believed Greenwood District was the future, their future. It felt like Eli had been protecting him, pushing him, and believing in him since he was a kid, and Jordan didn't feel ready to give that up. It hurt to think of her all the way across the country, where there could be no more cutting up and chilling back. No more jokes and secrets and discussions or afternoon adventures. He had felt confident that Eli's talent would be right at home here in Tulsa.

But, as he felt the heat from Eli's impassioned speech, Jordan knew it wasn't liquid confidence he heard. It wasn't the rum talking at all. He realized that he could finally hear her heart. Jordan took a deep breath and swallowed his little speech.

"I leave on the train tomorrow morning," Eli said in a low voice. The train might leave tomorrow, but Jordan knew Eli's heart had left the Greenwood District many years ago. He lifted his chin in quiet acknowledgment. When Eli slowly reached over and touched his hand, tears began to stream down both their faces. After an awkward silence, Eli attempted a lame joke, "Oh, you're not slick! You're just trying to make me miss my favorite movie of all time!"

"My lady, *The Green Monster* awaits …" Jordan bowed and used his best French gentleman's voice. "Would you please be so kind as to collect my shoulder bag over there?" he continued. As Eli turned to reach for the bag, Jordan sprinted off and yelled over his shoulder, "Last one to the corner sucks rotten eggs!"

"That's cheating, Jordan. Jordan! Wait up! That's not fair!" Eli protested loudly as she stumbled to her feet.

Jordan's peals of laughter and the sound of racing feet were his only response.

Jean

———◦♦◦———

*A nurse who avoids grieving a sudden loss
in the midst of
battling the deadly Spanish flu…*

Did you know that some researchers suggest that African Americans may have been less susceptible to catching the 1918 influenza virus? Perhaps segregation provided a protective bubble. Interestingly, pandemics disproportionately affect minorities, so the response during the Spanish flu was not the norm.

OCTOBER 19, 1918

Jean didn't know how she'd endure another day like yesterday. Her back wheezed in protest as she stood, slowly reaching to pull back the thin white fabric blocking the autumn light. With tears crawling down her worn face, Jean turned her back on the day. Her tired fingers caressed the letter still tucked deep inside the pocket of her pinafore. Memories of Cornell's mahogany skin and smoky voice tugged at her soul. She wouldn't let her mind go there. Not today. She averted her eyes from the folded American flag that marked Cornell's side of the bed.

Forget about all the things stolen by the war, Jean told herself. *I have to face today's battle because, with more than 650,000 casualties so far, this Spanish flu isn't taking any prisoners.*

6 MONTHS EARLIER

APRIL 17, 1918

It was the spring of 1918 when that first wave swept through Tulsa. *It was more of a brush than a sweep,* Jean reasoned as she adjusted the belt that held together her flowing dress and pinafore. She added an extra pin to the thick, coily hair she had twisted into an elaborate knot at the back of her head. Her nursing cap perched like a crown on her head. Jean did a mental check to make sure her surgical wares and identifying armband were in place before stepping outside her brick two-story home on Elgin Street. Her crisp uniform sounded like a harsh whisper as she strode toward Archer Street, where she ran a small clinic for the Public Health Service.

Seven days a week, Jean made her rounds of patients who were mostly elderly or homebound. As she walked by the tight rows of brick tenement homes each day, like clockwork, Ms. Ferguson would cackle her usual greeting.

"Looka this! Here comes the bee's knees!" Ms. Ferguson said with a grin-creased face.

"That's all you!" Jean replied. She noticed Ms. Ferguson had several folded kerchiefs nestled in her lap.

"What's ailing you?" Jean asked.

"Awl, it's just the 'fluenza," Ms. Ferguson said while exhaling a sharp cough.

"Well, I want you to get indoors and let your girls, Anna and Elizabeth, get some bone broth in you. Send Anna over to the clinic if the fever comes and lingers, ya hear?" Jean chided.

"It's going to take more than the 'fluenza to finish me off!" Ms. Ferguson said with more cackle than cough. Jean looked up to see Anna listening quietly from the narrow doorway. Anna looked at her mother with hopeful eyes before scurrying into the kitchen. Jean re-packed her medical satchel before heading out. She turned down Elgin, past Mount Zion Church, toward Brady Street. Soon she'd reach her next patient, old Mr. Harper, who lived with his wife and three sons. A breeze picked up; the sweet smell of hyacinths spiced the air. Her face lit up as a smile stretched into a grin. She quickened her stride as she approached the Harpers' residence. Jean pulled out the notepad and began to jot old Mr. Harper's responses to her questions about his amputated leg.

"Pains are not as bad today," old Mr. Harper said as a way of greeting.

"Well, that's something to be cheery about," Jean quipped in reply.

Old Mr. Harper's dark hair sat atop his grim face that was the color of ground nutmeg seeds. World War I had not been kind to old Mr. Harper. He left for France in the summer of 1917, and his unexpected return was the result of his leg getting blown off. It had been four months since he came home from being treated at Walter Reed Army Medical Center in Washington, D.C., where he had been promised a prosthetic leg. Corporal Harper banded together with other African American Army veterans to petition for the right to return home after enduring months of filthy living conditions in the medical facility. Although the band of brothers eventually made it home, the prosthetic leg remained a broken promise.

Unbidden, Jean's mind wandered to her husband, Cornell. *He's been deployed with a segregated labor force assigned to the American Expeditionary Forces aligned with the French and British along the Western Front in France. It's been a year since he left.*

Jean slowly shook the memories from her head as she looked into a face ravaged by pains that seemed amplified by each thud of the boys' running feet. The only reason old Mr. Harper and the other residents in her district could afford home health care was due to the government-funded health initiative funneled through Jean's clinic.

A hospital stay was a luxury that most Black and white people simply couldn't afford. With the help of pioneer nurses like Florence Nightingale and Lillian Wald, home health services were hailed as welcome solutions.

Jean was proud to be counted among the leading nurses in Tulsa. She served her patients by making sure their homes were clean, that lack of food wasn't an issue, and that they had whatever medicines they needed. Nobody could top Jean in an emergency. She could suture the deepest wounds, soothe the most stubborn fever, and even pull necessary herbs from the garden to make a potent salve if needed. She taught new mothers how to breastfeed and helped school-age kids learn to read. Jean sat with the elderly and offered respite for their exhausted caregivers. She didn't answer to nobody's physician and felt confident about whatever ailed her patients each day.

So, when Jean saw that more and more of her patients were coming in with the flu, she wasn't worried.

"Here, spit that into the bucket, Mr. Harper, and let me see how well your blood is flowing before I go," Jean said.

Her brown hands were guided by countless daily rehearsals as her mind did a tally of the number of patients presenting with flu-like symptoms this week. *Okay, there's Jepson and the Dandly's, Thurston and Mitchell …* As Jean's count topped 14, she paused to look at the tally she jotted on her notepad two days before. It stopped at four cases. Jean's brow furrowed as she made a mental note to refer to last year's records for a tally of influenza cases. It was time to get to the next patient's house.

One look at Sandra's sweat-beaded face and Jean instinctively knew she was facing another case of influenza. A wave of unease began to prickle at the back of her neck. Jean quickly moved through her patient checklist with a growing weight on her chest. Something was very wrong.

At the Archer Street Clinic, things didn't look much better. There stood a sprawling line of people waiting to enter the stark white building. Fever, fatigue, cough, and chills. The symptoms were consistent from person to person. The sheer number of suffering people presented its own set of challenges because the clinic wasn't stocked with enough supplies to meet the unprecedented demand.

Jean was grateful that, despite the higher volume, each patient's symptoms were mild and consistent with a typical bout of influenza. The death toll was two out of the ninety-three people who contracted the illness.

SEPTEMBER 22, 1918

A second wave of influenza made an angry gash on the world, and Tulsa was not spared its wrath. Jean did a quick survey of the mobile hospital recently set up in the center of the Brady Arts District. Jean and the staff of the Archer Street Clinic joined forces with the American Red Cross, which had brought its team of nurses and physicians to meet the growing demand for immediate, life-saving medical care. Friends and neighbors died by the day. In many cases, they died by the hour. Jean prayed quickly, but quietly, before gently draping young Anna Ferguson with a dirt-stained sheet. She was the virulent strain's most recent casualty.

A handful of white and Black nurses rushed from bedside to bedside, but the demand was just too great. The sick and feeble called out by the hundreds even as each day brought an unexpected twist and supplies dwindled along with the number of helping hands. Jean didn't see how they could endure another day without volunteers to haul bodies from inside and around the makeshift hospital. The stench of rotting remains overwhelmed even the smell of sickness and impending death that settled over the Arts District.

Jean hadn't slept more than 30 minutes at a time for weeks in selfless service to friends, neighbors, and strangers. She watched helplessly as their lungs filled with fluids that they no longer had the strength to clear from their bodies. Jean saw Mrs. Nancy Putnam, the banker's wife, sprawled on a cot. She reached out for Jean's hand. Just a few short weeks ago, this woman would not have been seen walking along the same street as Jean. None of that mattered here, where death's sting was felt by all. Jean gently cradled Mrs. Putnam's limp hand while she prayed for her safe passage into the Great Beyond.

Shelton

A returning Army veteran who wrestles with
his inner demons
while looking for purpose ... Yet his journey
takes an unexpected turn.

Post-traumatic stress disorder was formerly called "shell shock" ... it was a major mental health concern during World War I, just as it is today.

APRIL 24, 1918

When I stepped off the train, although I was still in motion, it felt as if the world had frozen in place. Men in tailored pin-striped suits and women in Mary Jane heels stopped to stare at me as I walked by. I suppose they'd seen a Colored man in a uniform before, but I guess it's not something you see every day.

We were required to travel in our uniform, and I took special pride in mine. I wore an olive-colored khaki jacket, and my Army garrison cap sat at an angle on my head. I took care to blacken my worn combat boots. They looked like every bit of the hell they've walked through. I grabbed my bags from the Pullman porter, and he smiled and tipped his hat. As I walked through the crowd, people continued to stare.

The fact is, there were very few jobs that they let us do in the war, but we served with honor to help the Allies win. We served just as good as anybody. Now I want these white boys to know that I can serve here, back home, just as well as anybody, too.

I could smell the oil fields and all those drills out there looked like somethin' that needed a few extra hands. All I gotta do is let them know that I served our country, and I'm sure that they'll be glad to have an Army vet lend a hand. I headed into town confident in my ability to tie down a job.

I've never been all that tall at five feet, nine inches. Not the shortest guy. Not the tallest guy. I've always been strong, but all that hard work during the war just made me tougher. And I've always been fast. We used to have races among the soldiers. I'm proud to say I never lost a single one. So, I figured if there is anything that needs to be done related to hard work, I can get it done.

On my first day back, I decided to take a minute just to walk around town, tryin' to get my bearings. T-Town has changed so much since I left. I mean, it was nice before the war, but it almost feels like a big city like New York or Chicago with all of the businesses and restaurants and stores. This place sure has changed. I just wanted to walk around a bit and see what I could see. Just take it all in, y'know? I walked all up and down Greenwood Avenue. Dapper men and fashionable ladies drove the wide streets in black Ford Model A and Model T cars. I could hear a multitude of voices laughing, jiving, and calling greetings in a chorus of sounds. The streets were thick with the bustle of business being done well. Three- and four-story buildings formed walls along both sides of the street; I took my cap off and stared up at them in awe.

I stopped in Economy Drugstore to grab a copy of the Negro-owned *The Tulsa Star*. Then I walked on up to mama's house on King Street.

It's almost as if I could smell the cornbread and fried chicken and turnip greens from around the corner. Mama had all the food laid out and prepared like I was a big-time war hero.

"Shelton, what was it like? And were you scared? Who were your friends when you were there?" she asked.

"Mama, one good thing was that John Woodrow was there with me for a while, but his unit went to serve in another place. I never saw him after that." My voice trailed off, and I looked away.

Many of the 380,000 Colored soldiers deployed in the Great War did the unsavory jobs the white soldiers wouldn't or couldn't do. Jobs like digging mass graves for flu victims and war casualties or digging trenches and latrines. We cooked and sewed and served. We also could be found in all regiments from the cavalry, infantry, medical, signal, artillery, chaplaincy, and engineers, just to name a few. We served as officers and enlisted. I mean, everybody knew about Benjamin Blayton, a Buffalo Soldier, who enlisted out of Lincoln County.

Although they placed us in segregated units, we often served eagerly and with valor. Many of my comrades told stories about not being given a hero's welcome when they came home. It was hard for them to face the fact that, although they were willing to die for the flag in another country, they still dealt with the hatred felt by white soldiers and other Americans.

I wasn't really in the frame of mind to think about the war. And I really didn't want to talk too much. All I knew was I hadn't had a good home-cooked meal in what felt like forever. Tomorrow, I'll think about everything else. But right now, all I know is that when the gravy from the turnip greens soaks up into the bottom of the cornbread, there's nothing in the world that could be more perfect.

When I woke up the next morning, I was ready to go. I didn't really know where to start, so I walked down near the train station and figured I would ask around about work at the oil fields. I stopped and tried to talk to the folks at the Oil Field Supply, Gypsy Oil, and Harvey Young Oil Company Yet, over and over, they all said the same thing.

"We not lookin' for no more help right now."

After all that walkin' and goin' back and forth and getting doors slammed in my face, I was really tired.

I don't know what the heck is coming over me. I started thinking about all my fellow soldiers from the war and all the stuff I had seen. I thought about Woodrow and wondered what happened to him. I thought about Sandy; he was the one American white boy who was nice to me the entire time I was in France. He got killed on the Western Front. I cried a lot when I learned that he had died. I had never felt this way before. Even though I was safe and sound back home in T-Town, suddenly, I was really sad.

So I walked over to Vaden's Pool Hall to get a drink. I just sat there after I finished my third round of whiskey. And then I decided to drink some more. *It feels like the death, bombings, and explosions are just all coming down on me at once.* My thoughts were like permanent stains on my brain. I couldn't escape them.

When I finally woke up, I had a real bad headache. I don't even remember how I got home last night. I just know that when I woke up, I still had on all my clothes. Only my shoes were off my feet. I don't even remember what happened over the course of the last few days either. *It's all a blur,* I thought. I could smell the coffee coming from the kitchen, so I dragged myself out of bed and down the hall to pour myself a cup. That's when mama came back into the room.

"Rough night, huh, Shel?" mama asked in a knowing voice.

"Yeah. I guess so," I grumbled.

"You want to talk about it?"

"No, ma'am. Not right now." I said, hoping she'd change the subject.

Mama looked at me intently before stating, "Harper asked about you."

"I'll go by and see him today," I replied.

By the time I got dressed, my head was still hurting a bit. But I felt a lot better. I walked down to Harper's house on Brady Street, and we just sat and talked about everything except his amputated leg.

We talked about the war, our friends we lost, and all of the barriers we had to face as Colored boys in the white man's army. We sat there and talked and drank and drank and talked. And that's when Jean came by.

I wasn't prepared to see her, and I definitely didn't want her to see me like I was. Jean was my high school sweetheart, but she married that ball player, Cornell, and that was that. I heard that he died in the war, too. So sad. We lost so many.

"Well, hello, stranger," Jean said as she sat her nurse's satchel on the chair.

"Hi, Jean," I said, hoping my words came out clear.

"That's it? Jus 'Hi, Jean?'" She teased. "Well, it's good to see you, Shelton. I didn't know that you were back."

"Yeah. There's no place like home," I said with a slight grin.

"Hey, Mr. Harper, you need to be more careful about the company you keep. This one here is trouble." Jean playfully warned as she began to pull her nursing supplies from her satchel. She was a nurse who had come by to tend to Harper and make sure he was comfortable.

I just smiled as I made my way outside to give him privacy. I was still sitting there on the front porch when Jean left. She slowed and looked at me with a discerning stare like she could see right through me.

"Are you okay?" Jean asked.

When she asked, I knew she wasn't *really* asking me if I was okay. She was actually telling me that she knew I was not okay.

"I'll be okay. I'm just looking for work is all," I confessed.

"You should go down to the Stradford Hotel. They're looking for help," Jean advised. The Stradford was an upscale Negro-owned hotel located in the Greenwood District.

"Okay, I will." I tried to sound reassuring.

The next day, I kept my word. I went straight down to the Stradford and asked if they were looking for help. The girl at the front desk told me to walk around back by the loading dock and ask for Johnnie D. Apparently, Johnnie D. is the supervisor for all of the maintenance and hospitality workers.

Johnnie D. took one look at me and asked, "Where did you serve?"

I told him, "Lots of places. Mainly Germany, Belgium, and France."

He said, "You're hired. When can you start?"

"Right now, if you want!" I said with a grin.

"Well, hop up here and help unload this truck. There's more than enough work to go around here."

I felt the really heavy weight suddenly lift off my shoulders. I'd never been so happy to do hard labor. It was a really good day. Later that day, I went back to Harper's house to see if he knew where I could find Jean. He said to check the Archer Street Clinic but that she probably wouldn't mind if I just stopped by her house.

"She lives in that brick house with the white shutters on Elgin Street," he said.

"Thanks, Harper!" I said, practically skipping away. I could hear him chuckle his reply.

It just so happened that, as I approached the clinic, Jean was coming right toward me.

"Well, hello again, stranger!" I said, as she looked up from the book she was reading as she walked.

"Oh, hey! Did you swing by the Stradford like I said?" Jean asked.

"I sure did. And guess what?"

"What?" Jean asked with a quizzical expression on her face.

"They hired me on the spot! I came here because I wanted to thank you for pointing me in the right direction."

"Sure. That's great! I'm so glad it worked out." She looked as though she was ready to walk right past me.

"You better believe it! Listen, I wanna return the favor. Can I buy you dinner?" I asked.

"I don't know. I'm very busy, and I still have clients to see tonight," Jean replied.

"Oh no, it doesn't have to be tonight."

"I don't know. We'll see," she responded.

"Ok. But for now, can I at least walk you home?"

She gave me a cautious look, and then she spoke.

"I suppose so."

It was a short walk, but it felt like hours. We laughed and talked about old times. Our parents were some of the first to come up to Tulsa from Mississippi. My entire family was from Greenwood, Mississippi. My mama and daddy had said that when they heard that this new town was called Greenwood, they knew it was God showing them their new home.

Jean and I strolled without a care, chatted each other up, and laughed 'til our sides hurt. *She's too young to be a widow, and she's still even more beautiful than I remember*, I thought.

∽

I worked hard over the last few months. Every day blurs together with loading, unloading, stacking, stocking, cleaning, and fixing. I don't think I even have a job title. But if it has to do with hard labor, helping fix things, and making things run smoothly, I'm the guy. The days are good—really good actually. It's the nights that are the problem.

I keep having these terrible dreams. Every night, when I sleep, I live out a different version of the same dream. I'll hear a loud bang, and then I'll see a dead body on the ground. Then I'll hear a rifle's sharp report and see another dead body. I'd hear gunshot after gunshot … Explosion after explosion. I see dead bodies one after another. Finally, the last dead body I see is mine. I always wake up when I see my body. But I always know all the others who are dead. They'll be dead in my dreams whether they actually died in the war or not. Like Harper. I'd see him in my dreams, but he's still alive. It's hard. It's like we all are dead. The war killed us.

Yet, all around me, life in T-Town seems to move on. The number of Colored folk moving to Greenwood continues to increase. It seems like another high-rise building is going up every couple of months. It's a good time to make money, buy land, and enjoy the nightlife. This is a good thing because my dreams have gotten so bad that I am afraid to go to sleep at night.

Sometimes the noise and music in the District are too much. At those times, instead of going into town, I stay awake and try to keep busy. I got my hands on a broken-down Model T that I am trying to fix up. I just go and work on that engine until I am too tired to lift another finger. But the dreams still don't go away. So I been drinking more to help me sleep.

I figured out that the more I drink, the less often I wake up from the dreams. As a matter of fact, when I black out, I don't even remember the dreams. The problem is the drinking is causing me other problems. Problems with Jean.

One Sunday morning, I made plans with Jean to go to the park for an early morning breakfast picnic. 'Cuz in the summer, afternoons are as hot as a brick oven. The problem is I had too much to drink on Saturday night. We were supposed to meet at 8 a.m., but I was unconscious and didn't wake 'til around noon that day. I dragged on some clothes and rushed in slow motion towards her house. She was sitting on the porch with tears streaming from her eyes.

I had planned everything I was going to say, but she wouldn't hear a word of it. She just spoke softly and quietly.

"I can't take it. I can't take it. I can't handle it. I can't handle the drinking. I can't handle the silence. I can't handle the missed appointments and moodiness. I know it's been hard for you, but it's been hard for me, too. It's been hard for all of us, and I can't take no more pain. I can't take no more grief. I can't take no more sadness. I just can't. I just can't take it no more." She let the tears run down her cheeks and chin and didn't bother to wipe away her grief.

I never said a word. I just sat there on the stoop; my sweat-soaked shirt still damp against my skin. Then Jean got up from her chair and went inside. The door closed with a bang. Months later, the sound still echoes through my mind like a shot fired across the battlefield.

Mary

<hr>

*A white American Red Cross official who
must make a harrowing choice ...
If caught in the act, the consequences could
cost her more than just her job ...*

In Oklahoma, it became difficult to track the spread of the cases of influenza. Jim W. Smith, an official in Oklahoma, reported that people would recover and then return to work before regaining full health. In actuality, people would relapse in the morning and be dead by nightfall. That is just how deadly the strain of flu was.

AUGUST 9, 1918

Mary Putnam walked downstairs, balancing a box of signs issued by the American Red Cross. She planned to deliver the signs to local shop-keepers per order ARC 5-32. The signs simply read, "In order to stop the spread of influenza, please phone in your orders, and we will call you for delivery or pick up."

Mary started volunteering with the Red Cross last year at the start of the First World War. As the daughter of a successful banker, she wanted to make a difference, but she would soon learn that she'd make her mark in unexpected ways. While she waited for William to pull the car around, Mary balanced the box of signs on one hip while twirling a few wisps of her rusty red hair with a finger. Mary could hear deep-timbered voices floating through the maze leading to her father's library. Curiosity pulled at her ears as she eased down the hall with the box still glued to her hip.

"This flood of darkies into Tulsa is what's causing the disease to spread like this," Mr. Putnam said with venom in his voice.

"Yes, it's the unsanitary, crowded conditions they live in and the various temptations they surround themselves with at the saloons. Despicable!" said the second voice.

Mr. Putnam fired back, "It's even in the papers. We can stop the spread of this doggone disease if we can keep those Negroes in their own area and out of the city."

Mary's pale skin flushed with anger. She wanted to burst into the room and tell her daddy, *Viruses don't discriminate against who they attack, but people do! People like you!* Just as she built the nerve to confront the two men, Mary heard the unmistakable click of her mother's heels on the hardwood floors.

"A proper lady does not meddle in the business affairs of men." Nancy Putnam held a sharp smile as she spoke. Mary knew her mother had already sized her up from head to heels, and she found her lacking.

Mary remembered the box of signs still balanced on her hip.

"Mother, I have to go into town to deliver these signs. William is waiting out front for me. I'll see you before dinner!" Mary slipped from her mother's watchful gaze and walked back to the foyer where William reached for her box. *It wasn't fair for Negroes to take the blame for everything that goes wrong in the world!* As she sat in the back seat, her mind searched for ways to even the playing field. *But how?*

"William, take me to Cherry Street by the bookstore, then over to Oklahoma Tire Supply so I can drop off signs."

William pulled out of the circular driveway in front of the Putnam's spacious estate. The quiet country road widened into the bustling Tulsa business district, which was lined by tall three- and four-story brick buildings. The black T-Ford eased to a stop in front of the tire supply store, and Mary hopped out to distribute her fliers. She marched into the store and plopped two fliers on the counter for Mr. McGee and explained how taking orders would slow the spread of influenza. While a clerk went to put the signage on the door, Mary slipped outside, eager to set her plan in motion. But first, she had two more stops: Roxy's Diner and Books for Less.

As Mary climbed back into the Model T, she instructed William to drive her to *The Tulsa Star*, a Negro-owned newspaper located in the affluent Greenwood District. William's gray eyes met hers in the rearview mirror. She tilted her head in a defiant response before he gave a quick nod and turned the car toward Greenwood Avenue.

Founded in 1912, *The Tulsa Star* was the definitive Democratic African American newspaper published by A.J. Smitherman. The paper provided a timely slap in the face to the dominant Republican papers that tried to silence Negro voices. Mary knew that *The Tulsa Star* was the hub from which information, ideas, and social issues were exchanged. She'd use her influential family name and position as a Red Cross official to push for social change. *Here goes nothing*, she thought as she gripped the box of signs seated on the black leather seat beside her. Mary's heart raced in her chest as William looked at her through the rearview mirror. Her legs felt frozen to the seat as she stared up at the glass doors leading into *The*

Tulsa Star. Mary's damp hands now clutched the cardboard box; beads of sweat formed along her hairline.

"On second thought, let's get the rest of these fliers handed out in the Arts District," Mary said to William.

William nodded in agreement and pulled out into the bustling city street.

SEPTEMBER 29, 1918

Mary sat with a team of other Red Cross officials, medical professionals, and Tulsa city delegates, including Mayor H.L. Hubbard. An emergency meeting had been called in order to slow or even stop the influenza virus, which had killed a staggering 500 white Tulsa residents in just the last six days. Mary took copious notes as Mrs. Frum argued that information and resources be spread to all city residents, not just the white ones. Councilman Turnkey immediately shot down the suggestion.

"We will not send *our* people into those neighborhoods where the filth alone can make us sick. Let the Negroes and Indians tend to their own," Turnkey said.

"But what about the many Negro Army veterans who have served our country and community with honor? They live there, too! And the Indians! They're already suffering from lack of food, education, and needed medical care!" Mrs. Frum shot back.

The city council quickly moved on to other matters. Mrs. Frum turned to Mary, Ms. Batey, and several other Red Cross volunteers and narrowed her eyes.

"We're not going to tolerate this, are we? We're not! This isn't over! We cannot let this wicked disease kill off Negro and Indian men, women, and *children*! The other officials shook their heads and lowered their eyes. But not Mary. Her eyes also flashed with a now-familiar defiance as she looked at the careful notes that she planned to give to Mr. Jeremiah Vader, a reporter for *The Tulsa Star*.

After the emergency meeting ended, Mary told William to drive her to *The Tulsa Star*. She folded the handwritten notes that she imagined would be of good use in *The Star's* next op-ed piece. Although Mary enjoyed seeing the burnt red flush of frustration on her father's face as he discussed *The Star's* latest flaming exposé, Mary wanted to do more for the Negro community than just funnel inside information. But when the car stopped in front of the news outlet, again, her resolve weakened. She directed William to head back to the estate.

OCTOBER 7, 1918

Today there was a second emergency meeting between Red Cross and city officials. Influenza was devastating the city and the world. The city was adamant about only supplying the white residents. In good conscience, Mary could not— would not— allow the city to deliberately withhold supplies and information from Negro families. Ms. Frum seemed to sense Mary's frustration, so she pulled her aside after the meeting.

Ms. Frum confided that she planned to stay at the Red Cross offices until closing tonight so that she could sneak much-needed medicine, food, and supplies to Nurse Jean at the Archer Street Clinic. Jean would then hand them out to the Negroes and Indians who depended on the local clinic for medical care. Whenever the ARC supply truck came to replenish the city, a small team would make sure the Archer Street Clinic got their fair share, too. Ms. Frum connected Mary with a logistics team from the O.W. Gurley Warehouses, which was owned by the most influential Negro businessman in the city. In the morning, Ms. Frum also planned to introduce her to Mr. Vader, the reporter from *The Tulsa Star*. The timing couldn't have been better.

The horse-drawn wagons, with their wares covered with canvas and hay, pulled away from the supply point. Mary locked the office doors and walked purposefully to where William parked the

Model T. She glanced back over her shoulder at the retreating supply wagon when the driver lifted his mahogany hand in a solemn salute. Mary clutched the handwritten notes from the emergency meeting in her damp hands and exhaled. Her real work has just begun.

Jeremiah

A former slave owned by Native Americans who learns more about the American dream than anyone ever believed possible …

Cherokee and other southeastern Native American nations had African American slaves. However, after the Civil War ended, Native Americans were required to emancipate their slaves. The former slaves of the Cherokee became known as Cherokee Freedmen. They were then allowed to become a part of the Cherokee Nation, which was in accordance with the 1866 Reconstruction Treaty.

Sarah Rector was a Creek Freedman minor who was allocated 160 acres of land, which was allowed by the Dawes Allotment Act of 1887. While most other former slaves received rocky and infertile land, Sarah's land happened to be located right in the middle of the Glenn Pool oil field, which was discovered in 1905. Sarah's father decided to lease his daughter's parcel of land to a major oil company, which helped pay his annual tax bill. A couple of years later, an oil driller struck oil that produced more than 100 gallons per day!

MARCH 23, 1900

*I*t was two to three weeks after the last frost. The sun was just warm enough, not yet high or hot on its perch in the sky. It was time to plant the corn. My wife's brown fingers dropped each kernel of maize into the little open mouths she had formed with the soil. Betty-Louise sang a rhythmic a cappella song that we used to synchronize our movements.

When my family settled in Ardmore in South Central Oklahoma, life was hard but good. We're the descendants of Indian slaveholders. When our people were finally turned loose, the Indians actually had to follow through on what the government said and give us 40 acres and a mule. Can't say the same for the Negroes who were finally let loose by whites.

"Jeremiah, I'm thinkin' the weather will hold 'til we get through," Betty-Louise said in her rich voice. I gave a grunt in reply. My mind was on other, more pressing issues. I couldn't stop thinking about what was happening in Tulsa.

☙

The Cherokees were the only of the five great tribes to let their slaves go in 1863 before the Civil War ended. My parents were among those who became freedmen that summer. Around then, things weren't exactly easy for freedmen. I remember my parents talking about how poorly Chickasaws and Choctaws treated their newly freed slaves. However, that wasn't anything new. During slavery, Indians often beat slaves and treated them with cruelty. Dark skin was looked down upon. Although white men could marry Indian women, it was forbidden to marry among the Negroes. It was shunned so hard that an Indian could be kicked out of the tribe for marrying a Negro woman. My older brother and me are living proof that an Indian man wouldn't get kicked out of the tribe for doing other things to a Negro woman. My loosely curled hair was the color of a raven's wings. My mother used to weave threads and trinkets into my hair when it used to flow past my shoulders. My skin shimmered dark, just like molasses, even while my eyes, cheeks, and jaw had the unmistakable cut of a Cherokee warrior.

Even for the Cherokee Nation, owning slaves was about power and political clout. The government had to come in and force the tribes to hand the freedmen equal rights, although the white man didn't abide by the same laws.

My family still tells stories of the Great Removal when the government forced more than 100,000 Indians to relocate across thousands of miles through nine southeastern states. Between 1831-

1840, just sixty years before, Indians were forced to leave millions of acres of their own land. Land that their ancestors had nurtured for generations before the white people stole it away.

My family was a part of that grueling and deadly march to new lands. We aren't strangers to hardship, hard times, or hard luck. So, although we were often treated with cruelty, we were able to learn valuable survival skills that helped us become ready for the day our own lands were signed over to us. We knew the Cherokees gave us our freedom, but they did not like having to give us their land and treat us as equals. The way they saw it, Indians now had these new lands, but the government overrode the Cherokee political system in order to force them to share with their former slaves. All this even while the white man didn't follow the same laws. "Outraged" didn't even come close to describing how the tribes reacted.

None of this stopped my parents from wanting more for our family. Once we were free, we got papers giving our family forty acres and a mule. The next thing my parents did was send me to a segregated school for the children of freedmen. My older siblings stayed on the ranch to work the land. We were bonafide tribe members, but we weren't allowed to attend the school run by the Quakers. In our area, there were seven schools. And by the time I was thirteen, the Cherokee Nation even had a high school. I remember looking around the small, poorly built building with old wood floors and a gaping hole in the wall for a doorway. I dared not smile openly, but I almost burst from excitement! I would soon learn how to read and write!

When I came of marrying age, my father signed over ten acres to me and each of my two siblings. They kept the other ten acres for themselves. When I found Betty-Louise and married her, my family had already helped me lay a good foundation on this farmland. The last five years have served us well. Yet, when news spread that Tulsa offered up new opportunities for people like me, I wanted to pursue them. It was as if my desire was a seed God planted in the soil of my heart.

MAY 3, 1901

In order to relocate to Tulsa, I told Betty-Louise that we'd use the money we made from selling five acres of our land to my siblings. Around this time, we made the acquaintance of E.P. McCabe, a settler and land agent out of Kansas. We heard that he was the first person to tell freedmen about the Black Migration. He wanted folks to head to the city he founded in Langston, Oklahoma, but I saw an even bigger opportunity in Tulsa. Oil was just discovered at Red Fork, and I knew in my soul that an oil boom would follow. I planned to be a part of it.

"Now, McCabe, if you can't help me broker a plot of land in Tulsa, then I'll have somebody else get it for me," I said.

"No need to threaten me, Jeremiah!" McCabe said with a smile that did little to mask his discomfort. "I'll get you what you need," he assured me.

McCabe secured a small plot of land in an area that would eventually become a part of downtown Tulsa. I joined oil mining teams and learned how to drill for oil and got a lay of the land. I could see that kerosene and oil lamps were becoming more popular and caught word that a new type of engine was discovered. One that burned fuel from inside the engine. Use of this type of engine would create a demand for oil unlike anything the world has ever seen!

"I think we have a couple years to figure out a way to get in on this boom, Betty-Louise!" I cried. She looked at me with bright almond-shaped eyes that matched my excitement. Our son, James, peeked from among her flowing, bright-colored skirts. His reddish skin seemed to shine in the glow of the lamp. The opportunity to make my mark came from an old familiar source.

Outside of the mining encampment, I overheard a few of the Indian merchants talking about an oil seep at a nearby stream. I already knew that the Indians used crude oil for mosquito repellent, tonics, and salves. The medicine man from our tribe would tell stories about how the black water was a gift from the Great Spirit. We even had a way to skim the black water. One that was passed down since the beginning of time. I knew finding an oil seep was the break I was looking for!

"If there are oil seeps, there will be an oil gusher," I explained to Jack Jones and Dee Hartmen, two Negro speculators from Arkansas. "If you can help me buy land nearby, I will find somebody to transport the oil when it's found," I said.

"Yeah, that's Creek land out that way," Jack said.

"We can get our guy to broker a lease for us. When the time is right, we'll sublease the land to all the other speculators who will flood the area," Dee said while flashing a wide-toothed grin.

I didn't tell the two that I already met a scientist who could process the raw oil and make it usable in the combustible engine, kerosene heaters, and lamps. If all goes according to plan, I'll be able to process oil for different uses, transport it, and sublease land to other speculators.

NOVEMBER 12, 1905

The sun hadn't yet peeped its head over the horizon, but I felt in my spirit that it was gonna be a good day.

I watched my Betty-Louise as she prepared to get dressed. She seemed to sense that I was holding my breath. She smiled shyly and reached for my hand. After everything we've lived through, we still found time to make eyes at each other. Before I could steal a kiss, she bopped me on the head with a feather-filled pillow! I laughed and tried to lunge for her, but she took off around the side of the bed.

"Betty-Louise!" I called out. "Paybacks, Betty-Louise! Paybacks are a comin'!" I said with glee in my voice.

She giggled in response before peeking her face back through the doorway in order to poke her tongue out at me.

"Betty-Louise!" I laughed again.

I looked in on our six-year-old son, James, who sleepily rolled onto his back. His arm flung over his face. In the bed across the room lay his four-year-old sister, Emma. Both had strong Cherokee features, but they were blessed with their mother's full lips. I didn't stop to pat their heads as usual. I needed to get to a meeting with a new land broker. A fella by the name of O.W. Gurley wanted to talk about oil and land.

My oil refinery business had really taken off as speculators still nursed the Red Fork oil mine. I created a system for transporting and refining oil that just couldn't be matched. I decided to take advantage of a recent law that had land "for Negroes only." I had already secured fifty-year land leases from fifty Creek Indian families. I also bought forty acres and planned to set up a dry goods supply store or something similar. Turns out, O.W. Gurley had the same idea.

"I just laid claim to my forty. We haven't been here long, but I'm opening up a boarding house for Negroes who want to settle here," Gurley said.

"I'm thinking I can send folks your way. Good men who are looking for work," I replied.

When talking to Gurley, I couldn't help but light up and dream bigger than before. The man is a true visionary, and he shared my belief that something big was in the air. After Gurley and I shook hands, neither of us could imagine that in the dark early morning, just 10 days later, our wildest dreams would come true. About a mile from my plot of land, the Glenn Pool Oil Reserve was discovered ... and it was a gusher! Almost overnight, speculators lined up to sublease the land we had already leased from the Creek Indians. Gurley's boarding house filled up so fast that he opened five more. As Tulsa's population exploded, some of the oil miners we hired went on to open other businesses to support the almost overwhelming demand for goods and services.

By 1906, Gurley called his forty acres "Greenwood," and other freedmen began using the rights allowed through the Dawes Act to acquire land in the same area. It quickly became a safe haven for other Negroes coming to Tulsa. I watched Greenwood evolve from a handful of shabby buildings to a boomtown that included banks, a newspaper, hotels, pool halls, luxury shops, nightclubs, movie theaters, and even a library.

I often parked my Model T, walked with my son down Greenwood Avenue, pointed out the newest sights, and reminded him that the future belonged to us. I knew one day the papers would write stories about all the freedmen and Negroes like us who made millions of dollars and built a beautiful city we all could call home.

"Son," I said while smiling into his bright eyes, "this place was built by us, for us. And can't nobody ever take that away from you. Look around! This is a reminder that greatness is within you, son! They can burn this place to the ground, but don't you let nobody ever steal your belief or dreams from your heart."

My throat grew tight as I looked down at my son. I kneeled until we were eye level, and I gripped his arms gently in my hands.

"James, I want you to promise me that you'll keep these words hidden in your heart," I said as emotion filled my voice.

James leaned in and pressed his forehead against mine. "I promise, Papa," he said with a seriousness beyond his six years.

I closed my eyes and, at last, let a smile spread across my face.

Julius and Marie

A grandson who goes on a walking
tour of the Greenwood District with his
grandmother, which not only reveals the
founders' stories but also a secret
about himself…

Ottowa W. Gurley, founder of Black Wall Street, was born on Christmas Day of 1868 to John and Rosanna Gurley (both freed slaves) in Huntsville, Alabama. The family relocated to Pine Bluff, Arkansas. After the Civil War, Black families quickly took advantage of their newfound freedom. Blacks voted just as often as whites and even held political offices from state supreme courts down to county courts.

$\mathcal{M}$y grandma is the strongest person I know. People call her Marie, but I call her Grandma. One of the reasons I know she is strong is because, when I was really little, I used to sit with her in church and play with her hands. Don't ask me why I did. I just did. I played with her hands. I would grab her hands with mine, and my hands always seemed so small; her hands were so big. I would stare at her hands. I'd look at the back of her hand and the inside. The back showed her pecan brown skin and the wrinkles from what looked like years and years of hard work in the fields back where she used to live in Huntsville, Alabama.

Her hands felt strong like she could use them to lift a whole automobile by herself. I held her big, strong hands with mine, and I don't know why. I just like her hands. Maybe her hands make me feel safe.

I think grandma might be a superhero. The pockets on her dresses hide many magical secrets! She always wears those same dresses with the colorful flowers on them. I think she might wear them because whatever she has in those pockets can even protect her from the bad guys, like the ones who took my mama and daddy away.

You want to know another way I know grandma is a superhero? She's very fast! When grandma is using her super speed walk, it's impossible to catch her. She yells back at me and says, "C'mon, boy, you gon' make me late for my appointment." She had on her flowery dress again, with thick black heels with the round toe, and a hat. It must be important because grandma only wears a hat when we go to church. She held her hat down with one of those strong hands, with the other hand, she reached back and grabbed for me. Then she said, "Julius, we can't be late! If we're late, I'm gon' have to wait a whole two months for another appointment."

I think grandma might have given me some of her super speed because, when I grabbed her hand, I suddenly felt a big power boost. And then I was moving faster than my legs could carry me. I want to be a superhero like grandma. When we made it to the big building downtown, grandma took out her face cloth and patted her face and neck. She was tired. *We* were tired. But I don't think we were late.

When we left the building, grandma was smiling. I guess we weren't late after all. Grandma said she would take me to get some ice cream. I like it when grandma makes ice cream at home. She lets me help, too. I get to turn the big arm that spins the wheel inside the wooden bucket. It's fun! And the ice cream is so good! But today, we get to buy some ice cream from the downtown shop.

Grandma got some gingersnaps and hoop cheese, and I got a chocolate cone. When Ms. Doris at the counter handed us our treats, she smiled and said, "That'll be six cents." I looked at grandma, and she handed me two shiny coins. One shiny penny and one shiny nickel. I passed them to Ms. Doris, and we said goodbye. We walked outside, and grandma looked up and said, "You see that building right there, son? That's the Stradford Hotel. When you grow up, you're gonna be a smart and successful man like Mr. Stradford."

"Who's Mr. Stradford?"

"Oh, Mr. Stradford is a very rich businessman, son. He owns the Stradford Hotel, which is the biggest and best around. He made it so that we Colored folk could have the same exact experience that white folks have down at their fancy hotels," grandma explained.

"One thing I like about Mr. Stradford is he believes that Colored people have a better chance of getting ahead if we put our money together and work together and support each other and our businesses," grandma said.

"So he went and bought up land and would only sell it to other Negroes. He sure did," grandma said while nodding her head.

"He didn't sell to any white folks, Grandma? Was that fair?" I asked.

"You doggone right it was fair," grandma said firmly. "After everything white folks keep doing to hold us down, we need a chance to just catch up." I could tell grandma was about to change the subject.

"You see this other building here?" grandma asked.

"Yes, Grandma."

"Well, right down there is Gurley Hotel. It was the very first commercial business on this street. I hear it costs like $55,000! Next to it are the Brunswick

Billiard Parlor and Dock Eastmand & Hughes Cafe," grandma said.

"You know Carter's Barbershop? Where you used to get your hair cut? Gurley also owns that entire two-story building. Hardy Rooms, a pool hall, and a cigar store are inside the building, too."

Mr. Gurley and Mr. Stradford are two of the most successful Colored men you'll ever meet. When Colored people started to come up from Huntsville, Mississippi and other places, it was because Mr. Gurley bought the land and invited a lot of us to come and make better lives for ourselves. It turns out, Mr. Gurley had good sense.

"You know, Mr. Gurley is from Huntsville, too, don'tcha? Some good, smart people come out of that city," grandma said with a wink.

"Now, after he bought all that land, Tulsa began to grow. More oil was found, and a great flood of people started moving here. We had to start a lot of businesses because the white folks wouldn't let us frequent theirs," grandma said with a frown. Then she seemed to brighten up a bit.

"Those Jim Crow laws tried to keep us down. I think white folk believe we can't survive without them, but we proved that wrong!" Grandma motioned to all of the buildings and the Black folks bustling in and out of them.

"We have all of this here—just for us—because it was Mr. Gurley and Mr. Stradford who loaned everyone money to help them get started," grandma said.

"Wow, Grandma!" I said in awe.

"Mr. Gurley and Mr. Stradford are heroes, son. Now, let me show you something else."

We walked down a few blocks and grandma showed me Booker T. Washington School.

"You know who Booker T. Washington was, son?"

"Wasn't he the president of the United States?" I asked.

"No, baby. George Washington was the president of the United States. Booker T. Washington was the president of Tuskegee Institute, a Colored training school in Alabama. He came to visit us here in Greenwood, and he said that Greenwood was a 'Negro Wall Street.' So, when they finished this school, they named it after Mr. Booker T."

Then we walked back down past the hotels. When we walked by Dreamland Theater, grandma spoke up again.

"Baby, you see that movie theater over there? I remember the day that theater opened. We were so proud to have our own Colored theater! You know, we weren't allowed to sit in the other theaters in town. We were only allowed to work there. But the day that our first theater opened, we finally had a place of our own where we could sit down and enjoy ourselves like civilized and important people."

"But why can't we go sit in the other theaters?" I asked as I stared up at the tall windows and tried to peek at the pictures of famous actors and actresses that were on the walls inside and outside.

"Well, baby, sometimes people have an idea in their mind that other people are less valuable or less important," grandma explained.

"But, Grandma, didn't God make everybody special?" I asked.

"Yes, baby! You're absolutely right. God made everyone special."

"So then how come we have to have different theaters?" I persisted.

"I don't know, baby … I just don't know," grandma sighed.

"But I will take you to sit in your own seat at *this* theater real soon," grandma promised.

"There isn't any sound playing during the movie. Ms. Bates plays the piano during the whole thing. She's behind something so she doesn't distract from the show," grandma explained.

That's when we walked by the Williams Building. And as soon as she saw the building, grandma started smiling really big.

"Oh, darlin', listen! This is the Williams Building. We came here from Huntsville with the Williams family. We only had one old wagon, and we had loaded everything we owned on that old wagon. We was all traveling together. Our family and the Williams family and two other families. We was traveling for about four days when the wagon granddaddy and I was in broke down. That old wagon was already in bad shape. But when we hit that bump, it felt like the entire wagon just gave up!" grandma said. She chuckled at the memory.

"It was far past fixing, but that didn't stop the Williams family from helping us. I don't know how they managed, but the Williams men somehow stacked all of our things onto their wagon right along with all of their things. And we made it all the way here to Oklahoma. Our families will always be close because of that generous deed. Then grandma pointed to a building across the street.

"See that office right there? That's Earl Real Estate. Remember I told you how Mr. Gurley bought all of that land and invited people to come and own some land and start some businesses? Well, Mr. Earl was the businessman that helped all of the Negro folk buy their properties free and clear.

"These men had a plan, and they worked their plan to perfection! These are powerful men, son. And I know when you grow up, you're gonna be a strong man, too. You're gonna be like Mr. Gurley, Mr. Stradford, Booker T. Washington, the Williams men, and Mr. Earl. You're gonna be strong like them," grandma said with a serious voice.

"You mean strong like a superhero, Grandma?" I asked.

"You know what, son? Yes. Strong like a superhero," grandma said. She sounded sincere.

After that, I suddenly felt … invincible! And then we walked the rest of the way home, smiling and eating our treats. I was even able to keep up without grandma holding my hand this time.

Annalie

A single mother of two who defies the odds
and learns new ways to turn the impossible
into what's possible …

There were other towns formed by African Americans. A lot of Blacks felt discouraged due to the failures of the Reconstruction Act, so they looked West. Benjamin "Pap" Singleton founded Nicodemus, Rattle Bone Hollow, Hoggstown, and many other towns in Kansas. He rallied a group called the "Exodusters." Thousands of Blacks who organized under Edwin P. McCabe formed and joined clubs in Oklahoma and worked to make it an all-Black state. They formed more than thirty towns. In 1897, McCabe went on to found Langston College.

The bell rang twice as Annalie leaned over to pick up the next sheet in the basket. She knew she'd have to press the clothes faster if she wanted to keep her new job with Ms. Winchell. The bell tinkled a third time, which signaled it was time to get to the floors in the upper bedchambers. Annalie usually counted to ten while she ironed to make sure the heat didn't scorch the freshly starched cotton sheets.

If I bring Bessie and Blanche with me tomorrow, I might can pick up another two hours of work since I won't need to rush home, Annalie thought. She smiled at the thought of her eight- and ten-year-old daughters even while her brow crinkled at her dilemma. *How quickly will I get the extra money I need to pay rent in two weeks?*

Annalie could expect to earn $900 a year if she didn't miss any cleaning days and continued to work nights at two of the boarding houses in town. On the weekends, she worked as a server down at the Cotton Club. The speakeasy was one of many hotspots in the Greenwood District that jazz and blues musicians called the Chitlin Circuit. Thanksgiving week on the circuit could net Annalie an extra $200!

Annalie would be able to pay all her bills if she did all her own laundry in addition to sewing her own clothes. Thankfully, she considered sewing her anointed gift rather than a tedious chore. With her kind of schedule, there wasn't any free time, down time, or family time. It was always time to work. If it weren't for Annalie's mom and dad, plus the girls' other set of grandparents, Annalie didn't know how she'd survive.

Annalie blinked back stubborn tears as she thought of the life that she left behind in Atlanta just four years ago. She had a happy life with her strong, wise husband, Moses. His presence was enough to fill a room. Oh, and his smile … Annalie couldn't help but soften as she saw his handsome face in her mind's eye. Moses was one to always stand for what was right, and it cost him his life. Those white men snatched Moses from not just her life but from the whole community down in Atlanta, where the couple had relocated ten years ago. The night after Moses was taken, Annalie packed up her and the girls' things into two stateroom trunks made of old leather and wood. The heavy iron base kept their personal items secure, while the tree sap coating kept everything dry during their exodus. Annalie and Moses' neighbor, Perlie, loaded the wagon that would carry the trio to the port where they'd load a steamboat headed back to her family's home in Tulsa, Oklahoma.

The five days spent on that steamboat were the worst days of Annalie's life. She blocked out the sound of crass men and the mooing and bleating animals. But she could still vividly recall the stench and filth she and the girls lived in each day. They were forced to survive outdoors in treacherous conditions. It was only God's grace that helped her navigate those five arduous days spent traversing the Mississippi and Arkansas Rivers. On March 12, 1920, Annalie and the girls arrived safely at their port in Illinois in order to board a train for Tulsa.

Annalie's grief tried to fight viciously against her responsibility to care for herself and her girls, who were just four and six at the time. Turns out, her will to survive outlasted the pain. She couldn't remember the number of times she asked God to be the hands and feet that guided her through each grief-riddled day.

Annalie pulled herself from her reverie in order to hustle down the hall to attend the next housekeeping task on her daily schedule.

The late nights and early mornings meant that life sure was hard for Annalie, but she believed what the Good Book said: "The joy of the Lord is my strength." She had her own special formula for making each day her best:

> *Find at least three good things to smile about.*
> *Find at least three things to laugh about.*
> *Find at least three people to compliment.*
> *Find at least three reasons to say "thank you."*
> *Find at least three reasons to say "I love you."*
> *Find at least three reasons to say "I forgive you."*

This formula is probably why everybody down at Cady's and Gurley's Boarding Houses knew Annalie as the most cheerful and hardworking person there. It didn't matter what time she came on shift; she always sported the now-famous pep in her step and a smile on her lips. Boarders could count on Annalie to sing out a bright and melodious, "Rise and shine, Sunshine! Let's thank God we made it to another day!"

Annalie's girls, Bessie and Blanche, would often hear their mama talk about the power of joy.

"Deep pain teaches you reasons to find death, but it can teach you how to live, too," Annalie said.

She had rooms at both Cady's and Gurley's since she often pulled the late shift as on-call manager. The title just meant she did more cleaning and troubleshooting than the other house staff! Well, since she would be up until the wee hours anyway, Annalie kept her sewing machine and supplies on hand so that she could work during her shift.

On this particular night, Annalie sat and sewed two dresses for her girls. Her movements were quick and sure. She taught them how to select fabric and only cut what they needed so as not to waste even a stitch's worth of thread. Annalie often bought a cheaper dress and re-fashioned it into a stylish showstopper of a piece. Her skill surpassed even the finest dressmakers in Oklahoma City. Ten-year-old Blanche and eight-year-old Bessie tried on their dresses and walked down the wooden stairs to twirl in front of the full-length mirror on the first floor. To their surprise, Mr. Gurley, the owner of the boarding house, was sitting in the foyer smoking his pipe. He looked up from his book, *The Red Record* by Ida B. Wells.

"My, my, my!" Gurley said as he lavished the girls with fatherly affection. "These dresses are gorgeous! Did your mom take you shopping today?" Gurley asked.

"No, sir, mama makes these dresses herself," Blanche said as she smoothed the front of her dress.

"My mama can make two dresses an hour," Bessie bragged.

"Is that right, little lady?" Gurley asked with surprise.

"She sure can!" Bessie said with more sass than she probably should have used.

"She sure can, what?" Annalie asked as she entered the foyer with her small sewing basket still in her hand. She smiled a greeting at Gurley as she approached the girls.

"Don't mind these little ladies, I was just coming to escort them upstairs for bed," Annalie explained.

Gurley chuckled at Bessie as she took another twirl around the room.

"Your young lady says you can sew two dresses an hour," he stated.

"Actually, I can sew three an hour. Sometimes four," Annalie said with a quiet confidence.

"Have you considered sewing suits? My tailor fell ill three weeks ago and hasn't fully recovered. I need five suits for a business trip in two weeks," Gurley explained.

"I can measure you tonight, or you can come by in the morning so that I can take your measurements. If you need those suits in two weeks, I'll have them for you this week," Annalie stated. "I can help you with fabric selection tomorrow."

"I'll pay any upfront costs. I just need you to write out your budget," Gurley said before walking toward the front door. "I'll see you before first shift ends," he said as he tipped his hat at the girls.

"Goodnight, sir," Annalie said.

❧

Three Saturdays later, down at the Cotton Club, Annalie worked her usual section of the speakeasy. She smiled and charmed her way around the room, making sure everyone she met was having a good time. Women wore deep red lipstick and sparkling flappers in colors ranging from sapphire blue and emerald green to white, rose gold, and charcoal black. Their slicked pompadours and waved do's bobbed to the jazz and blues melodies that floated around the room. But this Saturday was different.

At each table, there was at least one gentleman who asked if Annalie could make him a fine suit like the ones she made for Gurley. They wanted suits that were even fancier than his. Instead of taking orders for drinks and food, Annalie wrote down their suit orders. By the end of the night, she had twelve new customers.

Two weeks later, Annalie had thirty-eight customers. By the end of the month, Annalie had a waitlist of 128 customers! She had so much business, she decided to scale back her hours cleaning for Ms. Winchell.

In three months, Annalie was able to open her own shop on Greenwood Avenue. Not only did she manage the two boarding houses, but she also hired an apprentice and two seamstresses to help customers while she measured, cut, and sewed to her heart's content. If sewing weren't such a special gift, Annalie doesn't know how she could fit anything extra into her work week. However, in an age where store-bought clothing was more popular than the more pricey, custom suits and dresses, Annalie's Custom Tailored Goods business flourished.

Since Annalie knew the ins and outs of running a busy boarding house, she figured she might try her hand at opening her own. Instead of constructing a tenement from scratch, Annalie had her eye on an apartment building on the outskirts of town. She paid visits to some of the more prominent businessmen she often served at the Cotton Club and in her tailor shop. She put together a proposal, and only one out of the five potential investors couldn't resist. But that's all Annalie needed.

She planned to open a boarding house that also offered onsite laundry and tailoring services. But she wouldn't just wash the oil miner's clothing in a copper tub. She would have two washing machines on the property, which would allow her to charge more for a two-day service. This business idea was an instant hit!

The location of Annalie's Boarding House was at a junction of Greenwood Avenue where the sounds coming from the railroad tracks and factories didn't intrude upon the boarders' living quarters. Two of the eight rooms were dedicated to Annalie's growing laundry and seamstress business, while she rented the other six rooms to boarders who enjoyed a bed-and-breakfast-style living arrangement. The line of people would often spill out to the street as the word spread about Annalie's expedited laundry service.

Annalie began to hire more helpers to meet the growing demand from all three of her now fully ripe businesses. When she was poor, she didn't have the freedom to *not* work. Now that she was rich, Annalie decided to bask in her success by freeing up more time to spend with her greatest assets: Bessie and Blanche. Not only did she choose to do more of what she loved, but she decided that maybe it was time to make space for new love. The smell of hot cotton pulled Annalie back to the present moment.

"Remember to count to ten as you iron. It will help you avoid scorching the dresses' fine fabrics," she told her team of assistants before moving on to the next lesson.

Eddie

A WWI veteran who demonstrates his
commitment to sacrifice
even in the face of unexpected danger …

O.B. Mann was a Black World War I veteran who fought in the Meuse–Argonne Offensive, a major fight for Allied forces and the largest in American history. It was his gun that fired at the start of the Tulsa Massacre.

W.E.B. Du Bois followed the lead of Booker T. Washington, who advocated that the term used to describe Black Americans be changed from Colored to Negro in the 1920s. Black leaders felt that the use of "Negro" better represented intellectual, artistic, and political assertiveness. "Black" became the preferred term once the movement surrounding the word Negro lost steam.

MAY 30, 1921

I suppose it was a regular day just like any other day. I woke up and prepared to start my day the same way I always started my day. I got out of bed, washed my face, and pulled my black suit, white shirt, and black tie from the closet. I laid my clothes across the bed and went to the kitchen. Beverly was already cooking my usual breakfast: grits, eggs, toast, and sausage.

Sometimes I had to grab it and run so that I wasn't late for work. But not this morning. There was a strange stillness this morning. Everything seemed to be moving slower than normal, and I had time … lots of time. At least that's how it seemed.

I sat down at the table and took my time eating breakfast. Then I called my son's name. "Junior, did you take out that trash like I asked you to?" I paused before taking another bite of eggs.

"Not yet, Pop," he replied.

"Well, let's get to it then, son," I gently chided him.

"Yes, Pop," he said in a shy voice.

I finished my coffee and then headed back to the bedroom to get dressed. I went to pull on my suit pants and sat for a second, staring at the scar on my right leg. Seeing its angry sneer snatched me back to the day of the explosion. This is the most powerful scar in the world. It always reminds me that you can be here one second and gone the next. Like Willie. He was walking right next to me that day.

And then, suddenly, he was gone. All I remember was we were walking and talking and then, BOOM! … He was gone. I was completely disoriented; I couldn't see anything through all the smoke and debris. I searched and searched, but Willie was gone. Although I never got the chance to say goodbye, I'm thankful to be alive.

My legs are strong, but that battle scar is a trusty reminder. I pulled on my shirt and tied my necktie. I slid my arms through the sleeves of my suit jacket before picking up my hat and grabbing the newspaper and keys to walk out the door.

I held the paper but hadn't even looked at it yet. Had I looked, I would've already known what had Lawrence so scared.

∞

I love Greenwood! I'm proud of this town. I like what the Colored business folks have built here. I don't particularly love being a driver, but it's honest work and helps us to keep food on the table. Yeah, there have been hard times in this town, but there have been a heck of a lot of good times, too.

I can't help but grin when I think about the jive talkin' and bailing we do to distract from the fight we all deal with every day. Yeah, we have our fair share of issues, but what family doesn't? Having each other is what makes us roll up our sleeves and make the most of anything we face. We get together down at Moe's Place and laugh so loud the white folks can probably hear us for miles down the road. Me and Bev like to drop Junior at her mama's house so that we can dance all night at the juke joint before going 'round the corner to Miss Jessie's to play poker, dominoes, and bingo.

Whap! We like to slap the bones down on the table while we each take turns beatin' up our gums.

"You don't got nothin' in yo' hand. Ain't nothin' to the bear but his curly hair!" Al shouted in his deep voice.

"You tryin' to call my bluff!" I laughed.

"I might be crackin', but I sho' am facting! And gimmee thirty-five!" I added, slapping another domino on the table.

The room let loose another roar of laughter as Al marked my score. I got him whopped by fifty points now. I looked across the room to make long eyes at my best girl, Bev. She gave me a slow wink before leaning in to hear what Margie would say next. That girl sure did talk a lot, and she was always down with the latest news. And that's Saturday night.

On Sunday mornings, we head over to Mount Zion Baptist Church on North Elgin in Greenwood. We'd line up out front, seein' and bein' seen in our pinstripes and Sunday's finest. But that wasn't the best part. The best part was listening to Pastor Lyons, who always gave us a good word of hope. It felt like he took words from God's mouth and planted them right in my heart. I needed those words of hope more than anything because it took strength to face each Monday morning, where I dress up and go to work driving a white man around in his own car.

The most valuable possession that a man can have is his dignity. And I can say, I never lost mine. I fought for my country in the war. I take good care of Bev and Junior, and we're able to buy what we need and some of the things we want. My faith and my family are my first priorities. Now, I don't think we should lay down and let the white man run all over us, but we also shouldn't go looking for trouble.

☙

I was almost at the edge of Greenwood when Lawrence hailed me down. He was tall and skinny and carried himself with a bold confidence. But not today. He looked like he had just run from a fire.

"You look like you just saw a ghost, man. What's the matter?" I asked.

Lawrence saw the paper on the front seat of the car, grabbed it, and held it up toward me with both hands. And sure enough, there it was on the front page of the paper. Plain as day: "Nab Negro for Attacking Girl in an Elevator."

Then he said, "I just heard some white boys saying they're gonna string up that Rowland boy. That's when I knew I had to get some help."

"So what we gon' do, Eddie?" He asked me.

I could tell that Lawrence was worried and kinda scared, but I could also tell he had his mind made up. He was sure something was gonna happen to that boy, but it was all happening so fast. I didn't have time to think.

"I don't know, Lawrence. Let me figure this out," I replied.

Then I thought to myself that I could easily tell Mr. Boseman that an emergency came up at home and that I needed the day off. After all, it is his car. So, if it wasn't on his property or if I wasn't driving him around somewhere, he should always know where it is and why … or at least he should have a decent explanation.

"Listen, Lawrence, I'm gonna come back here. Don't you move. I need about 10 minutes to go talk to Mr. Boseman, and I'll be right back."

"Ok, Eddie. I'll be right here," Lawrence said while glancing around like his nerves were jumping.

When I got to Mr. Boseman's house, there was a crowd of white men standing outside. They were gathered around Mr. Boseman like they were having a meeting. I hadn't even parked the car yet when the group kind of parted like the Red Sea.

Mr. Boseman came walking out from the middle of the group and held his hand up.

"I won't be needin' ya t'day, Eddie." His voice sounded cold and gruff. We got some business we need to take care of here."

I have never seen that many men at the Boseman house and certainly not that early in the morning. No one said a word. They all just stared at me. That's when I felt for sure that Lawrence might be right about the Rowland kid.

"Okay, sir. Thank you, sir," I said as I waved in that extra nice and polite southern way.

I put the car in gear and backed away slowly. I was really careful to drive safely because I didn't want to cause a scene, but my mind and heart were racing up and down those streets.

By the time I made it back to the corner where I left Lawrence, he looked really worried. I could tell that he had smoked several cigarettes because I could see the filters crowded around his feet below the stoop where he sat. He was working on a fresh one when I pulled up.

"What we gon' do, Eddie?"

"I still don't know, man. I don't know. Just get in the car. We'll figure something out."

As we drove away, I told Lawrence what I saw at the Boseman place. He looked at me and his eyes got really big, and then he got quiet as if he was in a trance. It was like he was daydreaming. Or maybe it was more like a nightmare happening in broad daylight. I told Lawrence to stay in the car and sit tight.

When I walked in the house, Bev was cleaning the kitchen. I went straight to the bedroom. She called out. "Eddie?"

I needed to get my hunting rifle and as many shells as I could find. That's when Bev called my name again. This time she sounded concerned.

"Edward?" I was standing there loading my rifle stacking shells. "Edward Charles Goodman … just what do you think you're doing? What is going on, Edward?" Her chestnut-colored face was creased with worry.

"I don't want you to know any more than you have to, Bev. But I gotta go handle something."

"Edward! Please talk to me," she almost pleaded.

"Not now, Beverly. I want you and Junior to stay inside tonight. I gotta go."

I grabbed my small stockpile and strode toward the front door. My first stop was to see Stradford, Johnnie D., and a couple of the guys who work on the loading dock. They're all soldiers. They took one look at me and Lawrence, and they just knew. They dropped their boxes and hopped in the car. The vibe was tense and electric as we drove toward Johnnie D.'s house. Johnnie D. has all kinds of weapons. It's like he robbed one of those armories after the war. He grabbed three rifles and several boxes of shells, and we all piled back into the car.

During the drive, we all were silent. It was like being back on the Western Front. We knew what was coming even though we didn't know when, where, or what to expect. There's always a calm right before a storm—an eerie stillness right before the most vicious battles. Johnnie D. inspected and then loaded one rifle. He went through his mental check, then passed it back to Lawrence. He loaded the second rifle and passed it back as well.

This wasn't on our list of things to do today, but as men, we must defend our families and our communities. And while I never met the Rowland kid who got arrested, whose responsibility is it to protect Greenwood? Mine. Ours.

We were in the zone and hadn't even talked much about what our plan would be or how we would find the young man. We knew he was at the jailhouse, but we needed to get eyes on the situation. I knew how these things go. They might take him to trial really quickly and get a guilty verdict before anyone could even speak up for him or even before anyone even knew what was going on. Or they could haul him out of jail during the day or night, and we'd never hear from Dick Rowland again.

We decided to head to the courthouse first. When we drove around the building, there were already a couple of small groups of tense white men standing outside the old brick building. They looked like they meant to handle serious business. We knew that a group of armed Negroes would mean immediate trouble, so we parked around the corner on Main Street.

We each decided to perch up on the roof of a nearby building and wait until any of us saw something. I settled in on top of the courthouse. The clear afternoon sky barely offered any cover.

I hunkered down and low crawled with just my forearms. I quietly dragged my body across the roof to be careful not to be seen by the vigilant smattering of men gathering below. If a single white person saw us heading up to the roof, the makeshift plan would fall apart.

It didn't take long before more people started to gather outside of the courthouse. The word was obviously getting around. By lunchtime, there was a real crowd forming. The more people that gathered, the rowdier the crowd became. I was glad for our bird's eye view.

After a few more hours, there was a big commotion outside the front of the courthouse. It was hard to tell what was happening from the roof, but it appeared that some men had pushed their way inside. They were yelling and demanding that Rowland be handed over, but they got kicked out of the courthouse. By this time, the crowd made sure that the city officials knew they would not be calmed down.

"That boy's gonna pay for putting his filthy hands on an innocent white girl," one man yelled.

We held our positions until well into the evening. I was hungry and tired, but it was obvious that something was about to happen. There was an electric current building through the air, and I could see in my brothers' eyes that they also knew it was only a matter of time before we hit a melting point.

Some men began chanting, "Send the nigger out! Send the nigger out!"

The bad spirit in the crowd just kept growing and growing. It felt like hours had passed; my mind was in the zone because I don't even recall what happened before that moment. I squeezed my rifle close and shook the last bit of fog from my mind. In between the chanting voices, I heard the first gun explode. And that's when all hell broke loose. It was clear that it was going to be a very long night.

Michael

A racist white man heading to the courthouse in pursuit of revenge ...

Did you know that insurance companies denied claims of Tulsa Massacre victims? These companies determined that "riot exclusion" clauses exempted claimants from payouts. Despite this, victims tried, to no avail, to persuade the companies that the violence was due to the actions and negligence of law enforcement. Many filed claims, however, the only approval was to a white pawnshop owner for ammunition stolen from his shop during the riots.

MAY 30, 1921

"These niggers are getting too big for their britch-
es around here. You mark my words. I'll kill'em
all dead before I let'em touch my little girls."

That's what I said. I meant it then, and I damn
sure mean it now!

It was about 8:30 on Saturday morning. The night
before, everybody 'round town had been talking all
night about the nigger who had his hands all over
that girl in the elevator in the building downtown.
We heard that the guys were gonna meet at Tom
Boseman's place to talk about how we're gonna go
about gettin' our hands on that boy.

We heard tell that they got him down there at the
courthouse, and all we need is for one of our boys to let
us into the building. We just gotta get our plan together.

When I got over to the Boseman place, a lot of
the guys were already there. They all sat outside the
barn. The freshly painted red brick stood out from
the cobblestone on the old building. Cooter and his
cousin, Big Ralph, looked grim as they stood back with
their arms crossed in front of them. The hair on their
heads was slicked back under gray caps. Willie, Darryl,
and his oldest son, Charlie, were there, too. Half the
buildings downtown must have been closed because
all the store owners were all at the Boseman place.

There were several groups of guys talking by
themselves—kinda huddled up and together in their
small little circles. Their combined voices created a

buzzing sound that did little to slice through the tense air. That's when Tom Boseman spoke up and quieted everybody down.

"Now, it's important for us to not go jumping to conclusions. We still don't have all the facts of this case. We need to find out what happened."

This crowd wasn't gonna stand for all of Tom's smooth-talking and sermonizing.

"We ALL know what happened, Tom, and we're not gonna stand for it, not one bit!" Darryl blurted out.

"You're all wet, Tom! Don't we all know what happened? Those animals are trying to take our women!" Willie said to the nodding crowd.

"Yeah, Tom! You gon' let 'em have your wife and your girls?!" Cooter asked Tom even while his eyes locked onto each one of our faces.

Tom Boseman was trying his best to calm everybody down.

"Now, now, now! I'm not saying there isn't something that happened. I just think we all need to have level heads and handle this thing with the right measure of justice. That might mean we take matters into our own hands. Or it might mean we let the law handle that boy," Tom said.

Me and the other men began to grumble among ourselves. And it was right at that moment that Tom's nigger driver brought Tom's car up the long driveway. We all stopped and stared real hard at that boy and some looked like they were ready to tar and feather him - as if he were the rapist.

Tom spoke quickly, "I won't be needin' ya t'day, Eddie. We got some business we need to take care of here."

Once he drove away, Tom tried to take advantage of the distraction by saying, "Listen, we can't just go around killing innocent people."

Before he could say another word, a voice called out from the crowd. "Who said anything about innocent people? Didn't the *Tribune* say he attacked that girl and ripped her clothes? And if you ask me, they're all guilty! They want our women. They steal our jobs. More of them move here every day. They're taking over this town. Tulsa is going down to the dumps because of those bastards! We can't just let them take over like this!" The man said.

"Tom, for the love of humanity! You've seen *The Birth of a Nation* motion picture just like we all have. These animals are unintelligent and are clearly wanton and aggressive toward our women!" Jeb spoke simply but with a fire we could all feel. "What we do here is necessary to preserve our American values and maintain the proper social order. Without action in the face of such an insult against one of our own, Tulsa will fall, followed by the rest of our great nation!" Jeb concluded.

The crowd let out a roar of approval. Some men clapped.

Tom tried his best to reach the crowd, but it was getting out of hand and fast.

"Why don't you all let me go down there and talk to the sheriff?" Tom almost pleaded with us. "Sheriff McCullough is a good man, and he's reasonable," he said.

"Stop the dag blame stalling, Tom! You're either with us or you're against us at this point. It's time to go get some justice. Who's with me?!" Darryl asked.

It seemed like most of us were turning against Tom.

"Yeah, Darryl!"

"Yeah, Darryl!"

"Yeah!"

"Yeah, Darryl! We won't sit around and wait for them to take over our town and turn it into Little Africa. We gotta protect our families," one man shouted while pumping his fist.

I couldn't help but feel amazed. Tom Boseman is a guy that people listen to. He's a rich businessman, and people just usually follow his lead. Not this time and not today. These guys are fed up. We're fed up! After letting out a sort of battle cry, our group just kinda scattered. We were all quiet as we left, but we were also very serious and had our minds set on making something happen. It's like they had fire in their eyes. I had to admit, I did, too. These guys are right. We gotta protect our families.

We didn't talk about what we were gonna do, but we all knew what had to be done. I got back into my wagon and headed to the Barnham's house.

I went up the dirt road and stood outside. Grady and his nephew, Frankie, were already waiting.

"You ready, Michael?" Grady asked me.

"Never been more ready," I answered.

I was going to stop by my house and get my rifle, but Grady goes hunting almost every weekend. He's got more guns than I've ever seen. He tossed me a shotgun, and I snatched it out of the air with one hand. Then he handed Frankie a rifle. Frankie's only 17, but when you've been handling guns mostly all of your life, age just doesn't matter all that much.

By the time we got down to the courthouse, there was already a crowd forming. Some of the guys from the Boseman place were already there. No one was saying anything. We just stood outside, almost like we were all waiting for that thing to happen that would spark what needed to happen next. So we stood and waited. Some of the fellas started talking to each other, but even then, I could tell it wasn't time to make a move.

That's when Tom Boseman drove up and went to the courthouse door. The wide, black door was closed to him for what felt like forever. After a while, the sheriff came outside, and he and Tom talked for a few minutes. Then the sheriff turned his back on Tom and went back inside. Tom just kind of stood there staring at the door, then he strode to his car and seemed to drive off as fast as that car could carry him.

After the sheriff went back inside, a few of the people in the group started shouting, "Send the nigger out! Send that nigger boy out here!" Moments later, a few angry voices turned into all of our voices.

"Send the nigger out! Send the nigger out!" We yelled at the wide, black door. Soon we cursed that closed door.

There were more and more people gathering. And the more people who came, the louder it got. At around noon, someone tried to break through the front door! There was a bit of a shoving match between the sheriff's men and our guys near the door, but when it all settled back down, somehow, not one man had gotten in. And that boy didn't come out.

The only thing that seemed to change was that there were now more and more men with guns, and we were ready for some action.

I turned to Grady and said, "I can see that there's quite a few people inside the courthouse looking down outta the windows."

They seemed to be afraid of the crowd but not scared enough to actually send that boy out. One man tore his cap from his head and his red eyes looked like they'd pop clean off his face. But it wasn't just him. There were lots of red-eyed men ready to kill for what's right and fair. Back and forth we hollered and yelled, "Send the nigger out! Make him pay!"

By about four o'clock, our voices were hoarse and we were really heated. We paced in front of the brick building while others clamored at the windows and doors of the courthouse. Several of the strongest and bravest of our group tried to force the doors and windows. No luck.

"Hey! I think the sheriff is moving the nigger upstairs to the fourth floor!" Someone shouted from his perch at the window.

Did they think they could actually protect him? I wondered. Still no sign of Tom Boseman. I wondered where he went, but it was only briefly. It doesn't matter much at all right now.

"Make him pay! Make him pay!" The crowd took up a chant.

That's when Darryl ran up with his cap practically balled in his clenched fists.

"Hey, y'all. I just went over to Mildred's house to use the phone. You know, I dialed the number to the courthouse and guess what? Someone actually picked up the phone!!!"

The crowd erupted in laughter that echoed throughout the square. The men looked at each other with their jaws hanging to their chests. Their faces seemed to say, why hadn't I thought to do that?

"I told them just as plain as I'm tellin' y'all right now. We are going to lynch that nigger tonight!" Darryl spoke with a firm, loud voice.

I believe every word.

Everybody cheered as if we had just won the battle over the Tulsa County Courthouse. We all broke out in another round of chanting: "Send the nigger out! Send the nigger out!"

Then even louder: "We're gonna make him pay! … Make him pay!"

Now I'm not quite sure the exact time when it happened, but it was a couple'a hours later when things changed. I know that there were several people who had been fussing at the doors and windows all day trying to get in. Somebody even mentioned getting a ladder over to reach the higher windows. Then I had the thought that if you're going to go through the trouble of gettin' a ladder, why not just break a window?

I s'pose the ladder is a much more discreet option, but it appears that brute force won out because, soon after I had that thought, I heard a window break. Then someone came back around the building saying three of our people got in. After about fifteen minutes, those three guys got thrown right out of the wide, black front door and down those courthouse steps!

By about 8:30 p.m. I still felt really angry, but I was beginning to wonder about dinner. My girl made the best chicken and dumplings. I was thinking about the gravy and how it's not too thick and not too loose when Tom Boseman showed up again. He talked to a few people for a while. Darryl was one of 'em. It was like Tom was campaigning for mayor or something. He went from one little group and then found another little group to talk up. After a while, he walked up the steps of the courthouse like he wanted to talk to everybody all at once.

When he got up on those steps, everybody came closer. I almost thought they wanted to hear what he had to say. The only problem is they didn't want to hear what he had to say.

"Listen, everybody, this has all gone too far. We are all very upset, but we're going about this all wrong. I believe we just might be happy with the outcome if we all just go home and allow the courts to do their job," Tom said.

Someone shouted what we all were thinking, "Aww, shut up, Tom! Just get out of the way unless you wanna be hung right beside that nigger." I leaned in and looked closer and saw that it was my neighbor, Travis.

"Listen, people, it doesn't help us to start a riot in the town we've all worked so hard to build." Tom kept talking as if Travis hadn't interrupted.

"Who said anything about a riot?! Just tell them to send the nigger out, and everything will be just fine, Tom!" Travis' red hair bobbed wildly as he said his piece.

The two went back and forth for only the heavens know how long. Tom tried his best, but it just wasn't working. We were just too mad, too loud, and too far gone. That's when Sheriff McCullough came outside.

Hundreds of us pushed even closer to the steps. I pushed in 'til I could almost taste his breath in my mouth. It's like we were all gonna attack the sheriff himself! We screamed and were hungry for blood. Then the unexpected happened. I can't say a single one of us saw it coming.

An armed group of Negro men walked up like they were gonna be the heroes of some story. There were like a hundred of 'em. Big rifles held at the ready position. Their eyes didn't even blink. The cries of "Send the nigger out! Send the nigger out!" kinda died off in the wind once those Negro soldiers came walking up.

Sheriff McCullough took advantage of this. He looked in their direction and spoke right to those Negroes. We all looked in their direction. I felt fear mixed with sweat start to slide down my back. We didn't plan for this. I didn't plan for this. Dragging one nigger from the jail was different from startin' a fight with a hundred niggers.

I'll never forget that time when I was kid and challenged Eddie to a fight. I took one swing at Eddie, and it was like hitting a tractor tire. He never even swung back. He just smiled at me. Eddie drives for Tom now. Dang near everywhere I looked, it seemed like there were 1,000 Eddies staring down the barrels of their guns that were aimed straight at us.

The sheriff's voice took on a different tone as he tried to reason with the Negroes. They stared him down with steady eyes, but then one mountain of a Negro with skin like coal and arms the size of tree trunks stepped out from their group. He tipped his hat and gave the slightest nod to the men by his side. I actually almost missed it. But immediately, the Negroes began to slowly step back from the crowd.

Our heads whipped left and right as we tried to see if it was a trick or trap, but they looked like they were listening to Sheriff McCullough after all!

But seeing all those niggers felt kinda like when a good boxer gets hit and gets a taste of his own blood. He's even more ready to make the other guy pay for that! I reckon that's how we all felt in that moment. How dare those niggers come out here with their guns and think they could protect that boy from us! We own this town! The more Tom cajoled those niggers into walking away, the more restless we got.

I was closest to the courthouse steps but could see a bunch'a commotion at the back of the crowd. Some guys had started chantin' again.

"Send the nigger out! Make him pay!" they hollered.

Suddenly a gunshot went off. There was this awful calm. I reckon that calm is what it feels like when you find yourself in the center of a twister. You can look through the wind and see chaos blowin' around you. You know it's only a matter of time before the winds take you, too. But, for now, time feels like it's stopped.

I didn't have time to look to see where the shot came from. The crowd began this massive stampede away from the courthouse steps. Then, right after that, I heard what sounded like two or three more shots. The blasts sounded distant. Muted. I looked to my right and saw Grady lock eyes with mine. He was trying to say something, but I couldn't hear over the silence; I couldn't see past the darkness. I guess the eye of the storm isn't such a bad place after all.

Historical Facts

LITAN
MOTEL

1. The 1918 Spanish flu didn't actually originate in Spain. It first showed up in late spring. However, when a second wave hit during late summer, doctors noted how different it was from the regular flu. This strain of flu caused so much stress on the body and had a high death rate. Interestingly, it was seen in more young adults than any other demographic.

2. W.E.B. Du Bois followed the lead of Booker T. Washington, who advocated that the term used to describe Black Americans be changed from Colored to Negro in the 1920s. Black leaders felt that the use of "Negro" better represented intellectual, artistic, and political assertiveness. "Black" became the preferred term once the movement surrounding the word Negro lost steam.

3. Post-traumatic stress disorder was formerly called "shell shock" … it was a major mental health concern during World War I, just as it is today.

4. The Lincoln Motion Picture Company in Omaha, Nebraska was founded by George and Nobel Johnson in 1916. Aimed at African American audiences, it was the first all-Black movie production unit in America. The company created five films, which were shown in Black churches and assembly halls.

5. Did you know that some researchers suggest that African Americans may have been less susceptible to catching the 1918 influenza virus? Perhaps segregation provided a protective bubble. Interestingly, pandemics disproportionately affect minorities, so the response during the Spanish flu was not the norm.

6. Ottowa W. Gurley, founder of Black Wall Street, was born on Christmas Day of 1868 to John and Rosanna Gurley (both freed slaves) in Huntsville, Alabama. The family relocated to Pine Bluff, Arkansas. After the Civil War, Black families quickly took advantage of their newfound freedom. Blacks voted just as often as whites and even held political offices from state supreme courts down to county courts.

7. In Oklahoma, it became difficult to track the spread of the cases of influenza. Jim W. Smith, an official in Oklahoma, reported that people would recover and then return to work before regaining full health. In actuality, people would relapse in the morning and be dead by nightfall. That is just how deadly the strain of flu was.

8. Cherokee and other southeastern Native American nations had African American slaves. However, after the Civil War

ended, Native Americans were required to emancipate their slaves. The former slaves of the Cherokee became known as Cherokee Freedmen. They were then allowed to become a part of the Cherokee Nation, which was in accordance with the 1866 Reconstruction Treaty.

9. O.B. Mann was a Black World War I veteran who fought in the Meuse-Argonne Offensive, a major fight for Allied forces and the largest in American history. It was his gun that fired at the start of the Tulsa Massacre.

10. Sarah Rector was a Creek Freedman minor who was allocated 160 acres of land, which was allowed by the Dawes Allotment Act of 1887. While most other former slaves received rocky and infertile land, Sarah's land happened to be located right in the middle of the Glenn Pool oil field, which was discovered in 1905. Sarah's father decided to lease his daughter's parcel of land to a major oil company, which helped pay his annual tax bill. A couple of years later, an oil driller struck oil that produced more than 100 gallons per day!

11. Did you know that insurance companies denied claims of Tulsa Massacre victims? These companies determined that "riot exclusion" clauses exempted claimants from

payouts. Despite this, victims tried, to no avail, to persuade the companies that the violence was due to the actions and negligence of law enforcement. Many filed claims, however, the only approval was to a white pawnshop owner for ammunition stolen from his shop during the riots.

12. There were other towns formed by African Americans. A lot of Blacks felt discouraged due to the failures of the Reconstruction Act, so they looked West. Benjamin "Pap" Singleton founded Nicodemus, Rattle Bone Hollow, Hoggstown, and many other towns in Kansas. He rallied a group called the "Exodusters." Thousands of Blacks who organized under Edwin P. McCabe formed and joined clubs in Oklahoma and worked to make it an all-Black state. They formed more than thirty towns. In 1897, McCabe went on to found Langston College.

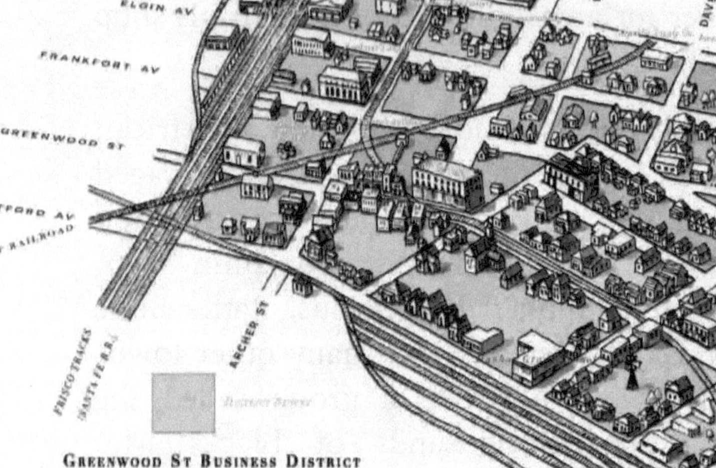

GREENWOOD ST BUSINESS DISTRICT
"BLACK WALL STREET"

ADDRESS	BUSINESSES	VALUE (Adjusted for Inflation)
1. (102) WILLIAMS BUILDING	I. Williams, Confectioner Dr. McKelvea, Physician	$12,500 ($188,500)
2. (108) BRYANT BUILDING	Bryant's Drug Store C.L. Netherland, Barber	$15,000 ($226,300)
3. (112) GURLEY BUILDING	Brunswick Billiard Parlor, Gurley Hotel, Dock Eastman & Hughes, Cafe	$55,000 ($830,000)
4. (120) DIXIE BUILDING	Dixie Theater, Samuel Strankenshet, Shoe Shiner. J. R. Bell.	$50,000 ($754,000)
5. (122) SMITH BUILDING	Welcome Grocery. Dr. Wells, Anderson, & Travis & Enterprise. Attorney E. J. Sadler. Y. M. C. A. Rooms Elliott & Hooker, Clothing and Dry Goods.	$30,000 ($452,000)
6. (126) HILL'S BUILDING	Tulsa Star, A. J. Smitherman	$30,000 ($452,000)
7. (202-208) REDWINE BUILDING	Wm. Kell, Druggist Red Wing Cafe, J. L. White Adolf Fuschle, Tailor, Red Wing Hotel, Mrs. J. T. Pressley Barber Shop, Abner & Hutton, Prop.	$8,000 ($120,000)
8. (102) E. G. HOWARD BUILDING	Barber Shop, Safety First Loan Co Mrs. Sarah Whitaker, Rooms	$12,500 ($188,500)
9. (111) PHILLIPS	Hardy & Hardy, Restaurant Harris St Harry, Rooms.	$15,000 ($226,300)
10. (115) PHILIP'S BUILDING	Castro's Barber Shop, E. A. Hardy, Furnished Rooms Gentry, Nerly & Vanes, Billiards Osborne Cigar Store.	$12,600 ($190,000)
11. (121) GIST BUILDING	T. F. Gist, Barber Nails Brothers, Shoe Repair Shop Gist Rooms	$12,500 ($188,500)
12. (123) GOODWIN BUILDING	Union Grocery, Duncan & Clinton	$7,000 ($105,500)

ADDRESS	BUSINESSES	VALUE (Adjusted for Inflation)
13. (127) MRS. TITUS BUILDING	Little Pullman Cafe	$1,500 ($22,600)
14. (129) WILLIAMS' BUILDING	Dreamland Theater, A. J. Whitley, Physician, Alexander Hotel	$7,000 ($105,500)
15. (201) MRS. PARTER BUILDING	Cain's Cafe Dr. R. T. Wotzer, Office	$7,000 ($105,500)
16. (301) STRADFORD HOTEL	Stradford Hotel, A. L. Freeman, Davis	$125,000 ($1,885,000)
17. VERNON CHURCH		$6,500 ($98,000)
18. (501) CLEAVER & CURRY BUILDING	Anderson & Preson, Groceries Knights of Pythias Odd Fellows Hall	$8,000 ($120,600)

Tales From the Greenwood District

Well before the race massacres of May and June 1921, the Greenwood District of Tulsa, Oklahoma comprised one of the most prosperous Black communities in the United States. Home to about 11,000 residents and hundreds of businesses, the backbone of the neighborhood was the eponymous Greenwood Street (now Avenue), known more colloquially as "Black Wall Street." Here neighborhood residents not only bought their groceries, shined their shoes, had their hair cut, and satisfied other quotidian needs; they established veritable institutions in banking, hospitality, manufacturing, entertainment, media, health care, and more in the name of developing a self-sustaining economy independent of the rest of white-majority Tulsa. The genuine entrepreneurial spirit of this enclave was indicative of the American Dream at that particular time, and it was a national beacon of inspiration for many other Black communities. Such unquestionable success is evident in what lay in the ruins of the neighborhood after the massacre; one appraisal by the American Red Cross conservatively estimated that property losses amounted to over $4 million—about $60 million adjusted for inflation 100 years later.

By

THE MAP DIVISION AND **DOOMSDAY BANANA, LLC.**

@THISISNOTREALE   @IDEAWINGMAN

*Hand illustrated with pen and ink
with digital text in May 2021*

SOURCES

RESEARCH

...ua Oklahoma, 1915 by
... (Library of Congress) (1918)

...merican Section, 1921" by
...rk Service (2016)

...nfolded" by
...ger for The Tulsa World (2020)

Events of the Tulsa Disaster by Mary E. Jones Parrish (1921)

"The Black Experience of Tulsa, Oklahoma" by J. Valdez
on storymaps.arcgis.com (2020)

"Black Wall Street and the Business of Creating a Community"
Retrieved from TicTocLife.com (2020)

Blackwallstreet.org

Black-Owned Businesses

This is a sampling of actual descriptions for some of the Black-owned businesses that made up the Greenwood District.

	Name	Address	Comment
Business			
	Woods Bldg.	North Greenwood Street 101 Earl Real Estate Co. 103 ½ Bayers & Anderson, Tailors 103 ½ R. T. Bridgwater, Physician 103 ½ T. R. Gentry, Real Estate 103 ½ Wesley Jones, Physician 103 ½ Tames M. Key, Physician	2-Story Brick Bldg. Value: $15,000 Size: 70x80

		103 ½ Mrs. Mary E. J. Parrish, School 103 ½ Two Apartments 103 ½ Theo Baughman, Oklahoma Sun Office	
	Williams Bldg.	North Greenwood Street 102 Dr. J. J. McKeever 102 Mrs. Lulu Williams, Confectionery 102 Second Floor Apartments 102 Third Floor Offices	3-Story Brick Bldg. Value: $12,500 Size: 25x35
	Mrs. E. G. Howard's Bldg.	North Greenwood Street 107 Barber Shop 107 ½ Safety First Loan Co. 107 ½ Mrs. Sarah Whitaker, Rooms	2-Story Brick Bldg. Value: $12,500 Size: 25x80
	Bryant Bldg.	North Greenwood Street 107 Dr. A. F. Bryant, Bryant's Drug Store 108 ½ Rooming House 110 C. L. Netherland, Barber Shop	2-Story Brick Bldg. Value: $15,000 Size: 50x90
	Phillip's Bldg.	North Greenwood Street 111 Hardy & Hardy, Restaurant 111 ½ Hardy St., Hardy Rooms	2-Story Brick Bldg. Value: $15,000 Size: 25x80

	Gurley Bldg.	North Greenwood Street 112 Brunswick Billiard Parlor 112 ½ Gurley Hotel 114 Dock Eastman & Hughes, Cafe	2-Story Brick Bldg. Value: $55,000 Size: 50x140
	Philip's Bldg.	North Greenwood Street 115 Carter's Barber Shop 115 ½ E. A. Hardy, Furnished Rooms 117 Gentry, Neely & Vadel, Billiards 117 Oquawka Cigar Store	2-Story Brick Bldg. Value: $12,600 Size: 50x80
	Gurley Bldg. O. W. Gurley.	North Greenwood Street 119 A. S. Newkirk, Photographer 119 ½ S. G. Smith, Insurance 119 ½ Sashears & Franklin, Attorneys and Oil Deal 119 ½ Smith's Apartment	2-Story Brick Bldg. Value: $10,000 Size: 25x60
	Dixie Bldg. Redfern	North Greenwood Street 120 Dixie Theater 120 ½ Samuel Stokenberry, Shoe Shiner 120 J. R. Bell	1-Story Brick Bldg. Value: $50,000 Size: 50x130

	Gist Bldg. Gist	North Greenwood Street 121 T. P. Gist, Barber 121 Nails Brothers, Shoe Repair Shop 121 ½ Gist Rooms	2-Story Brick Bldg. Value: $12,500 Size: 25x80
	Smith Bldg.	North Greenwood Street 122 Welcome Grocery 122 ½ Smith's Apartment 122 ½ Dr. Wells. 122 ½ Dr. Robinson 122 ½ Dr. P. Travis 122 ½ Dr. Smitherman 122 ½ Attorney E. I. Sadler 122 ½ V. M. C. A. Rooms 122 ½ Elliott & Hooker Clothing and Dry Goods	2-Story Brick Bldg. Value: $30,000 Size: 50x120
	Goodwin Bldg.	North Greenwood Street 123 Union Grocery, Duncan & Clinton 123 ½ Rooms	2-Story Brick Bldg. Value: $7,000 Size: 25x80
	Williams Bldg.	North Greenwood Street 129-133 Dreamland Theater 129 ½ A. J. Whitley, Physician 129 ¼ Alexander Hotel	2-Story Brick Bldg. Value: $7,000 Size: 25x80

	Mrs. Titus Bldg.	North Greenwood Street 127 Little Pullman Cafe	1-Story Brick Bldg. Value: $1,500 Size: 20x30
	Mrs. Partee Bldg.	North Greenwood Street 201 Cain's Cafe 203 Dr. R. T. Motley, Office	2-Story Brick Bldg. Value: $7,000 Size: 15x40
	Hill's Bldg.	North Greenwood Street 126 Star Printing Co., A. J. Smitherman 126 ½ Morgan Rooms	2-Story Brick Bldg. Value: $8,000 Size: 25x70
	Redwing Bldg.	North Greenwood Street 202 Wm. Kyle, Druggist 204 Red Wing Cafe, J. L. White 206 Abble Funche, Tailor, 206 ½ Red Wing Hotel, Mrs. J. T. Pressley 208 Barber Shop, Abner & Hutton, Prop.	2-Story Brick Bldg. Value: $8,000 Size: 25x70
	Stradford Bldg.	North Greenwood Street 301 Stradford Hotel 301 A. L. Ferguson, Drugs	2-Story Brick Bldg. Value: $50,000 Size: 50x140

	Cleaner & Cherry	North Greenwood Street 501 Anderson & Person, Groceries 501 ½ Knights of Pythias 501 ½ Odd Fellows Hall	2-Story Brick Bldg. Value: $8,000 Size: 25x80
	Burnett's Bldg.	Frankfort Avenue, North 302 T. J., Wiseman, People's Tailoring Co.	1 ½ -Story Brick Bldg. Value: $6,000 Size: 40x80
	Baker's Bldg.	Frankfort Avenue, North 304 W. A. Baker, Grocery 304 ½ Apartment	2-Story Brick Bldg. Value: $4,500 Size: 40x80
	Mrs. Meeks' Bldg.	Frankfort Avenue, North 525 Johnson's Plumbing Office 527 Bell & Little Cafe 529 Cold Drinks and Cream Parlor	1-Story Brick Bldg. Value: $750 Size: 25x40 1-Story Stone Bldg. Value: $5,000 Size: 25x100 1-Story Frame Value: $350 Size: 15x30

	Stradford Bldg.	Cameron, East Blacksmith's Shop Loup's Plumbing Office	Facing Cameron St. Included in Hotel Bldg. Waffle House

Author Bio

Julian B. Waddell is a thought leader in cyber security and a seasoned start-up strategist with a vast array of experience in both fields. That is what most people know about him. What you may not know is that he is a terrible singer and dancer, but that doesn't stop him from singing embarrassingly loud and at random while performing dance moves that look differently in his head than they do in real life. He is also a gifted storyteller with a passion for learning little known historical facts.

In order to fulfill his passion for entrepreneurial endeavors, he stepped down as the chief information security officer at Oakwood University to focus on being a professor and start-up consultant for early-stage entrepreneurs. Well, that's partly true. The more accurate reason was that he hadn't had time to play video games for years because of his dedication to the job. The moment he realized that he had significantly improved his organization's security posture, he knew it was time to dust off the old PS4 and ride off into the sunset.

Outside of all the awesome games he is currently playing, Julian is a great business wingman. Be it a grappling hook, a sound business plan, or X-ray vision, Julian works tirelessly to equip his clients with the tools they need to run successful businesses.

What makes Julian so good at what he does? He is an empathic critical thinking strategist who has 23 combined years of experience in information security, information technology, and business strategy. He has served as one of the lead technical specialists of the Data at Rest Security Encryption initiative implemented by NASA (They are in charge of getting us to space, PEOPLE!) to increase information security for their users, and his team received national recognition for their efforts. There is a lot that can be said about Julian "The Idea Wingman" Waddell, but there's not enough time in the world. If you ever get an opportunity to meet this living legend in person, ask him to tell you about the epic project he is currently taking on, challenge him to a game of Brawlhalla, OR congratulate him on becoming a published author. (This book is his first.)